Abraxas

The Haywire Halloween

Cinsearae Santiago

ABRAXAS: The Haywire Halloween

Cover Art and Design by C.R. Santiago

Published by Lulu Press

Author's acknowledgement: *I also want to give a big "THANK YOU!" to Brenda Scott for letting me use her awesome, 'flaming pumpkin' image on the cover. That pumpkin was* ***really*** *kick-ass!*

All photographs within the text by the author.

www.lulu.com/gratistavampires **Author's Bookstore**
http://BloodTouch.Webs.Com **Official Author Website**

ISBN: 978 0 557 06031 3
1st printing

Printed in the United States of America

ABRAXAS
The Haywire Halloween

Cinsearae R. Santiago

Praise for "*The ABRAXAS Series: Books 1-3*"

"I found myself drawn into Ms. Santiago's dark tale. The Abraxas Series offers a different slant on the paranormal; it hits the ground running and keeps the reader enthralled. The characters are well rounded; the story telling will keep you in suspended anticipation. It leaves you wanting more. Highly recommended!" **~Corvis Nocturnum, Author of "Embracing the Darkness; Understanding Dark Subcultures"** ***and*** **"Promethean Flame"**

"These days, the world appears virtually awash in vampire tales, so many of them of-a-piece that sometimes it's hard to remember if you've read the story before! Consequently, it's not just a relief but a true joy to read Cinsearae Santiago's unique ABRAXAS series. Her protagonist Christine Vargas is sharp and sassy and tells it like it is, even though she is caught in a world of darkness. Christine is a refreshing no-nonsense character, afraid of neither the living nor the undead, and full of down-to-earth integrity. If you love your vampire fiction full of conflict and romance, I recommend that you give the ABRAXAS books a read."
~Nancy Kilpatrick, Author of "The Power of the Blood" series and "The Goth Bible"

"My first thoughts of this book; absolutely, freaking amazing...This is definitely a book for someone who is in touch with their bad side, and can appreciate the sexy, gothic side to life... If you are someone who is not afraid to read spicy material and allow your blood to heat up, then get cozy and read this book!" **~FrontStreetReviews.com**

"An engaging and supernatural tale. Exotic and erotic." **~Mario Acevedo, Author of "The Undead Kama Sutra"**

"Each book builds in intensity until the story explodes off the page and makes you eager for more...Romance is mingled with suspense and creepy situations, making this a gripping read. Sinister and attention grabbing, The ABRAXAS Series will definitely keep you entertained." **~Nights and Weekends**

"Ms. Santiago adds a few new twists to the ever popular vampire genre and gives it a unique spin all its own. The way the story ends is a total surprise and very creative if not macabre." **~BittenByBooks.com**

"This is an engrossing and often extremely violent tale...The characters are well written and come to life on the page, and there is a great deal of action throughout the tale, as well as a moving love story." **~Coffee Time Romance**

"Now THIS is what vampires should be all about...Hot, sexy, brash, violent and ghastly...this is the type of vampires I want to read about...the kind that truly scare the crap out of you, make you want to be them...Move over vampires kings, queens and underlings...a new ruler has come to play (take over more like) and her name is Cinsearae Santiago. Realistic and cruel...I had so much fun being "had" by this book. Can't wait to be had again..."
~Andrea Dean Van Scoyoc for Twisted Dreams Magazine

"...A unique story based on the vampire legend." **~Night Owl Romance**

"Ms. Santiago created a world more interesting than just a typical vampire story that we have all come to know and love...This world is built and based around a family of vampires. Her characters are amazingly drawn out into this world, where the humans, witches and vampires collide. The plot of the story kept getting thicker and thicker, when you thought they were through with the fighting - you turned the page and you were wrong! Something was always around that dark corner to jump out at you! This was and is going to be on my fave's list!"~**Ruthie's Book Reviews**

"...I absolutely love how descriptive this book is. I actually felt like I was a part of all the action scenes. It was almost as if I was watching a movie rather than reading a book....I enjoyed the love story like any other romance novel, the paranormal flare only added dimensions to it....I can sincerely say that I am looking forward to reading the next book in this series. My attention was definitely intrigued." **~Shaprice, Reviewer for RWA Bookclub**

"The Abraxas Series *is, to me, a fresh new spin on the Vampire Legends; it is a humorous, fast paced collection of stories that far surpasses some of the Vampiric novels I've read in recent times."*~**Carrie White, Writer and Reviewer for FourStarRating.zxq.net**

The ABRAXAS Series: Books 1-3

ISBN: 978-1-4357-2847-9

Available now through

www.lulu.com/gratistavampires

Also available at the author's bookstore:

ABRAXAS: Seeing Green--Book 4

ISBN: 978-0-557-07369-6

Get it now at

www.lulu.com/gratistavampires

Edward lies in a coma in the hospital, with Christine having a sneaking suspicion that Ryan has something to do with Edward's current condition. Ryan continues to act strangely possessive of Christine to the point where it becomes too scary for her to deal with. His sexual forwardness doesn't make matters for her easier, either.

Edward's spectral form cries to Christine for help, as the clan soon discovers that Ryan's odd behavior is not his own...and to make matters more trying for her, Christine's best friend stops by for a visit, unknowing of her situation.

ALSO COMING SOON

ABRAXAS: Judgment
Book 5 in the series

The waters are getting testier when Christine and Ryan have to face the remaining Elders of their House to assess the progress of their Abraxas Clan, which someone has purported to be too chaotic and disorganized since Christine's arrival.

Magdalene, Kain's mate, passes a special bit of judgment all her own when she offers Christine a 'present' that will test her faith, love and devotion to the Abraxas Clan, as Christine is sent back in time---before she became a vampire.

ABRAXAS

The Haywire Halloween

1

"Dude, where's my skull?" Jonathan asked, as he wandered around the tea room with a queen-sized, black satin sheet draped over his arm. Kim, Kurt, Kiera and I watched him in mild amusement as he looked under the chairs and couch, getting flustered. "Where's my *skull*?" He repeated louder.

Kurt snorted. "Sittin' on your neck," he quipped.

"Oh, ha-ha," Jonathan retorted. "Really, though. You see it anywhere?"

"Nope," Kiera replied, checking her reflection in a compact mirror. "What do you need it for anyway? As if I need to ask."

"I'm gonna take it with me when I go trick-or-treating!" He grinned at us.

We stared at him for a moment, and Jonathan shrugged his shoulders. "What?"

"Do kids even *do* that anymore?" Kurt mumbled to himself.

"Uh, no self-respecting, nineteen-year-old goes *trick-or-treating*," Kim said, unwrapping a *Snickers* bar. "You should be checking out a party or something."

"Parties *suck*." Jonathan frowned. "Besides, I don't get invited to any."

"Wonder *why*." Kim rolled his eyes.

"Go to *Dracula's Ball*! Or even *Henri David's Halloween Ball*! There's *oodles* of stuff to check out in Philly. Plus, there's South Street too!" Kurt offered.

"I agree with Kurt," I said. "You look a *little* too big to be begging for candy at strangers' doors." Kiera patted his back in support as I continued. "You're gonna stick out like a sore thumb being an extra three feet taller than the rest of the kiddies."

Jonathan slouched, and let out a puff of air. “I guess you have a point, but what’ll I do now?”

“Just bask in the merriment of the night---like you always do.” Kiera slipped on a gold, lame’ jacket that looked like it was straight out of the sixties. The jacket went along with her paisley, pink and purple mini-dress and white go-go boots. “As for me, I *am* going to a party.”

Jonathan made a noise of annoyance, pointing to her as he looked at me. “See?! Invited! Me, *not* invited!”

“You have to *socialize* more, it’s the only way,” Kim said. At the word ‘socialize’, Jonathan cringed in terror and hissed at him.

“The *‘s’* word is just as bad as any four-letter word to me,” Jonathan spoke in a dark tone. “Agoraphobic, remember?”

“But you said this is your favorite time of the year,” I mentioned. “The only thing holding you back from enjoying the night, is you.” I gave him a gentle but knowing look as I put a hand on his shoulder. “If it’ll make you feel better, *I’ll* walk around with you.”

“Hey, I will too,” Kurt said and grinned.

“Count me in!” Kim chimed.

“Awww, Kodak moment!” Kiera gave us a group hug. “Yes, get him out of the house, *please*. As for me, I’m gone. See ya in the morning!”

“Oh, wait a sec, Kiera! Before you go, I got a present for ya!” Jonathan started up the stairs, then stopped. “Actually, I got a present for *both* of ya.” He smiled at me before running the rest of the way up.

I gave Kiera a quizzical look, and she held a hand to her forehead, groaning.

“He got us *presents*?” I asked her.

“Jonathan gave me a Halloween ‘present’ last year,” she said and sighed.

"Was it jewelry or something?"

"Yep. This tacky, *hideous* pair of skull earrings!" She leaned into me. "Ugh. Trust me, whatever he got you, it'll be something you can wear *only* for Halloween."

I snickered. "Well, it's the thought that counts, right?" She groaned again in response.

Jonathan ran back down the steps and stood in front of us, still smiling. "I checked out this little kiosk at the mall---"

"I went with him so he wouldn't go screaming through the crowds; don't worry," Kim said with a smirk. Jonathan cut him a look.

"*Anyway*, I saw some pretty cool Halloween jewelry, and thought about you two," Jonathan continued. "Kiera, I know you like purple, so this one is yours." He put something in her hand. "And I thought the one with leaves looked pretty neat for you," he said to me, putting something in my hand next.

It was a bracelet. The green and yellow glass beads were *perfectly* color-coordinated for the Fall season…

But then I saw the wacky-looking skull head that was also part of it. It kinda threw the whole bracelet off.

"*Wow*, Jonathan…" I said, swallowing quickly, giving a quirky grin. "That was so sweet of you! Thank you." I gave him a hug. Immediately, I put it on for his sake. I think I understood Kiera's lament. She was *still* staring at the bracelet in her hand.

"Gee, Jonathan…um, thanks." She gave a big, cheesy smile.

"Ya gonna put it on? It matches your outfit pretty well," he replied, looking eager.

She gave another little noise, and put it on. "Alrighty, *now* I'm gonna go. Catch you guys later." She blew us all a kiss and waved.

Once Kiera locked the door, Kim, Kurt, Jonathan and I

gave each other blank looks. Then Jonathan sighed.

"I *still* want my skull."

After fifteen minutes of more searching, Kurt found the thing under Dino's bed. Frowning, he handed it to Jonathan.

"Remind me to give that boy a *thrashin'* the next time I see him," he said to me. I held my hands up in defense. Dino had a way with getting under Jonathan's skin, and we all were wishing he'd stop his mean antics.

"Whoo-hoo! Let me go slap some white makeup on my face, then we can go!" He passed the skull to me, ran halfway up the steps, then stopped, looking at us funny. "You guys aren't dressing up?"

The remaining three of us looked at each other. "Well, if we were actually *going* somewhere, I *might* have," I said and shrugged.

"Me too," Kurt replied. "I was dying to try on that *Wonder Woman* outfit I saw in the costume store on Columbus Boulevard."

"*Really*, Kurt? *Wonder Woman*?" I put a hand on my hip.

"It was either that or Dr. Frankenfurter from *Rocky Horror*."

"Hm," Kim said. "I was thinking about being Eric Draven. You know, from *The Crow*."

"Ooo! Maybe I should do *that*," Jonathan said cheerfully, jumping up and down on the step.

"I'm curious though, what exactly *are* you?" I glanced at the skull in my hand, then at him again. "You're wearing a black sheet, covering your face in white makeup, and carrying a skull. I'm clueless. Death? The Headless Horseman?"

He shrugged. "Nothing really. Just some creepy-looking person with a skull."

Kurt folded his arms. "How inventive. That required *no*

creative thought at all. I expected *more* from you."

"I didn't *know* what to be!" Jonathan answered in his defense. "Unless I steal Kim's idea."

"You gonna finally paint over your *Clockwork Orange* eye tattoo so you can match your *Crow* one?"

"Let's just *go* man," Kim interrupted. "Time's a-wastin'!"

Jonathan continued going up the steps and was back down again in ten minutes, looking absolutely *awful*. But, he was happy, so that's all that mattered.

Jonathan had on one of his well-worn, Marilyn Manson t-shirts, black jeans, his favorite chucks, and the black satin sheet tied around his neck. A small portion of it was draped over his head like a hood. His face was a pasty white, and he gave himself the sunken-in, 'panda eyes' look. Last but not least, I could see he had spray-painted his hair *completely* purple. I gave him his skull and he tucked it under his arm, proudly smiling at us.

Kurt gawked at him. "Boy, you look like a hot, stir-fried *mess*, with some ***burnt*** oven-roasted mess on the ***side***, you hear me?"

Kim nearly choked on his second piece of candy from laughing so hard at Kurt's remark.

"Well, *you* try to throw yourself together in ten minutes!" Jonathan folded his arms, forgetting he had his skull under his arm. It fell to the floor with a *thunk*.

"Let Jonathan do what he wants. It's just for a night," I said, trying to keep the peace.

Jonathan ran to the kitchen next, the black sheet flapping behind him like a corny superhero. He returned with a wrinkled, plastic grocery bag.

"You really *are* gonna attempt to go trick-or-treating?!" Kim asked.

"*Only* if I see a group of kids. And if they're really

short, I'll get on my knees. The cape will hide my legs. Strategic, huh?"

I copied what Kiera did, and patted his back as a reply.

Believe it or not, Jonathan's little scheme worked on an entire two blocks, until one kid in the group ratted him out. As payback, Jonathan sprayed him in the face with silly-string, and dropped a stink bomb in the kid's candy bag before he took off running back towards us.

"That little weasel!" Jonathan huffed, then held up his bag, almost halfway full. "But I did good for just two blocks, huh?"

"Yeah, you *did*," I answered, peeking at his loot. "You don't happen to have a *Snickers* bar in there, do you?"

He rummaged through the bag and took out some bite-sized versions, putting them in my hand.

"Thank you," I said and smiled, unwrapping one.

The four of us continued down the street, Jonathan smiling all the way as he walked a few yards ahead of us.

"Dude is like nineteen going on nine," Kim whispered.

"And we all know *why*, so no need to get into that," Kurt replied.

"It just pisses me off how some smart kids get treated like shit sometimes," I spat. "And the repercussions for *him*..." I shook my head in remorse.

"It's always tough getting him into extra-curricular things *outside* of clan business…except around this time of year," Kim told me. "He always says he feels most comfortable around Halloween. October's his favorite month, naturally."

"Well, one stinking month out of a whole year is *not* enough time for someone to feel comfortable in their environment."

"Which explains why he's creatively crazy the *rest* of the time," Kurt answered. "It's how he copes."

Still walking ahead of us, I watched as Jonathan stooped over to pick up something.

"Whoa! *Cool,*" he said, slipping a necklace of some sort over his head.

"What'd you find?" Kurt asked him.

Jonathan turned around and faced us, holding out the pendant.

"Pretty awesome, huh? Someone must have lost a part of their costume."

It was a skeleton key. *Literally.* Silver in color, it was topped with a skull head, and on black, leather cording.

"Oh, yeah!" Kim started. "I think I saw something like that in one of the Halloween stores around here."

Kurt frowned, reluctant to touch it. "Why's it gotta look all menacing?"

"'Cause it's a *Halloween* accessory, *duh*!" Jonathan rolled his eyes. "You know---evil, creepy, spooky? It's *supposed* to look menacing."

"You know what skeleton keys represent, right?" Kurt folded his arms.

"Yeah, um… the way to unlock hidden doors, I think."

"You've got the general idea," Kim said. "They're objects that unveil mysteries, secrets, even the meanings of dreams. But if you ask me, some things *need* to be kept locked up."

Kurt flipped the pendant over, reading something inscribed on it. "*'Unleash your dreams and desires'*." He then gave Jonathan 'the crazy eye'---his infamous, one-eye-open-wide-and-one-eye-squinted look. "That's some creepy soundin' shit for just a cheesy, Halloween accessory!"

"You'd be surprised, Kurt. *Lots* of Halloween accessories aren't as crappy-looking as they used to be. Some stuff I wear year-round!"

"We've noticed." Kurt smirked.

"C'mon, I'm not done just yet," Jonathan continued, picking up the mood. "Maybe I'll try one more block or two, when I find another group."

A few stores in the surrounding areas were also handing out candy, giving older kids the freedom to take some, which Jonathan was relieved about. He was wondering whether or not he'd have to squat down again to look smaller, which, being his size, was proving impossible. Even Kim took a couple of pieces out of the plastic grinning pumpkin sitting on top of the store's counter. The boy had a pretty big sweet tooth.

"See? Isn't this more fun than going to a party?" Jonathan chirped.

I smiled. "Well, *I'm* having fun. It's kinda nostalgic. I haven't done this since elementary school."

The guys remained silent, not answering him.

We kept walking for a while, the little kiddie groups having vanished. We saw some older ones, around ten or twelve years of age, still wandering about. One of them actually toilet-papered a tree. It was in front of an abandoned house, so no actual harm was being done to someone's property. The kid laughed as he chucked the roll up into the tree; a long, white, fluttering streamer sailing high into the air until it got tangled in the branches for a moment, before dropping back down to the ground. He grabbed it, starting his antics all over again.

Kurt was pretty irked at that. "You should be using that toilet paper to wipe your ass, not decorate a tree!"

Startled, the kid turned around. He flipped Kurt off, and laughed.

Kurt was taken aback and gave a high-pitched gasp.

"Little snot-nosed, rat-bastard," he grumbled, motioning like he'd just kicked a ball.

Up the street, it was the kid who received the energies of

Kurt's gesture, getting the kick squarely up his rear end. The kid yelped, holding the seat of his pants, looking around in a panic. Seeing no one, he took off. Kurt giggled to himself.

I gave him a look. "C'mon now, you know we're not supposed to use our powers for stuff like that."

"Kinda like how you used them at the Christmas Ball last year?" He raised his eyebrow at me in knowing.

My face felt hot. "Touché," I said, smirking. "*Totally* different scenario, though."

We passed by an ice cream parlor that sat along a busy strip of boutique stores on the upper end of Germantown Avenue in Chestnut Hill. It wasn't too far from the place where Kiera and I had gotten our dresses for the Ball. The parlor didn't look like it was giving away candy, but Jonathan put his hands on the window, ogling the different kinds of ice cream.

"Dude, it's not hot enough to eat that stuff," Kim said.

"I *know*, but still, I wish I could have some, *anyway*."

A young girl in the store happened to spot Jonathan, waved at him, then came towards the door with a small cup in her hand.

"Hi there!" she said, handing him the cup. "My boss wasn't giving away anything for the trick-or-treaters; he's such a grump! But since I'm closing shop, I just couldn't let you pass by without giving you *something*." She smiled at him. "Happy Halloween!" She waved at us before closing the door again.

"Thank you!" Jonathan said, bouncing on his toes. He looked at us, wide-eyed, then stared at the ice cream as if it was the best thing in the world. "Wow, now *that* was awesome!" He scooped some ice cream out with the little wooden spoon she provided, then pointed it at me. "Want some?"

"No thank you, sweetie. Kim's right. It *is* a little too chilly for that."

"Never too chilly for me," he replied, putting the spoon

in his mouth. "*Mmmm.*"

Jonathan bounced ahead of us a few yards before maintaining a walk again. "Maybe if you guys had dressed up, she'd have given you some, too!" He called to us.

"That's alright," Kurt replied, waving it off. "I wasn't in an ice cream mood."

"Whoa! Check out that little cemetery over there!" Jonathan pointed to a churchyard a block away from us. "Let's go see!" He darted ahead, his candy bag hitting his leg with every step he took.

"Poor Jonathan," I said to myself. "I wish there was a way to help break him out of that *thing* he has. I worry how that will affect him when he gets older."

"Chicks aren't gonna take him too seriously, that's for damn sure," Kurt started.

"Only the shallow-minded and self-centered ones," I said. "If someone *really* cares about Jonathan, they'll understand and overlook his quirks."

"And he's got a *ton* of 'em," Kim quipped.

We caught up with Jonathan at the churchyard. He was standing in the center of it, spinning around in place, arms out, smiling, his head tilted up at the moon.

"Dude's gone batshit *crackers*!" Kim gawked at him, eyebrows raised.

"He's just enjoying himself," I said. "Let him. It's not often we get to see him smiling."

"Anyone would think he was locked away for a *looong* time and just got released," Kurt told me.

"Well, in a way, he *has*. The only time he goes anywhere is with you, right?" I looked at Kim, and he nodded.

"If I don't drag him out of the house, he's content just being up in his room, sometimes on that damn computer of his for *hours*."

"And I tried to get him to come to the club with me a

couple of times," Kurt added. "After the third try, I gave up. Too much of a sensory overload for him."

"Not to mention that little drinking problem he had," Kim said in a shifty tone, grinning. I looked at him.

"*What* drinking problem?"

"He just got one too many drinks in his system, that's all. He had his pants to his knees and was twirling his belt and a sock in the air, shuffling across the dance floor, going 'whoo-hoo!' everywhere. We had to pull him out," Kurt answered with his best straight face possible.

I slapped my hand over my mouth. "No way."

"Yeah, way!" Kim laughed. "His socialization skills are shot to hell."

"But how'd he even *get* the drinks? He's only nineteen. You have to be twenty-one to drink!"

"He actually used his vampish charms on one of the bartenders," Kurt answered. "I didn't even realize it until it was too late. He was already on the floor doing his little dance by the time I was notified. The patrons got a real kick outta watching Jonathan act like a fool."

"You *told* her that?!" Jonathan yelled at us, weaving through the grave markers as he approached us. "You guys *suck*! I told her *I'd* tell her that story!"

"It's just between us…and the patrons who saw," Kurt said with a grin.

"Ohhh, *that* was the story!" I exclaimed. "They were just trying to pass the time until you were done." I gave Jonathan a sad look. "I'm *so* sorry that happened to you, though!"

He sighed. "That was a baaad night for me." He looked to the moon. "Ya know, if I had one wish, I'd wish that *every day* would be Halloween! That way, I'd never have to worry about being uncomfortable in public places *ever again*."

Kurt sniffed. "That's a pretty tall order, kiddo."

I put my arm around his shoulders in sympathy, hugging him to me.

"Yeah," he said, sounding glum. "But could you imagine how *cool* that'd be?"

A strong gust of wind chilled us to the bone, making the hairs on my neck rise. The gale was so forceful, it sounded like moaning as it passed us, but *nothing else* had moved from the effects of the wind. No branches, no dead leaves, no litter on the ground. It was too freaky, to say the least.

"Did you notice that?" I whispered.

"Uh-huh," Kim answered.

Kurt looked all around us very carefully. "What in Hell's bells was *that*?"

"A spirit maybe," Kim replied, rubbing his chin. "A very restless one."

"No way," Jonathan said, shivering. "*That* strong?"

Everything was eerily silent at first, and it was only nine-thirty. *Way* too weird.

A shriek pierced the silence. Then another. And *another*. Next, we heard the screech of car tires and the metallic *boom* of its collision with something. The sound of shattering glass made my skin crawl. Nervous, we looked at each other again.

"What the fuck--?" Kurt looked towards the direction of the sounds.

My heart raced. "Jonathan, you're done, I hope. Maybe we should get back home."

He pointed in the direction Kurt had looked at, giving me a wide-eyed expression. He had a way of speaking to me without saying a word, and I knew *exactly* what he wanted to do. Check it out.

"Curiosity killed the cat, man!" Kurt put his hands on his hips.

Jonathan pointed to the sounds of the commotion again, looking at Kim this time. Kim caved in and sighed.

"Well, aside from his curiosity, what if some folks are in trouble? We could help."

I slapped a hand to my forehead. "You're right. Okay, let's go."

Kurt was mumbling something under his breath, but I only caught part of it.

"---Don't feel like investigating this dumb, spooky shit. We ain't *Scooby Doo,* or *Nancy Drew…*"

More screams. We picked up the pace. Now back on Germantown's main street, we saw several things amiss.

Horribly amiss.

The first thing we spotted was a guy face-down on the sidewalk, a smashed pumpkin beside his head.

"Oh…my…*God*! If he got walloped by *that…*" Kurt said as we rushed to the guy. We stared at him for a moment, not quite sure if what we were seeing was for real at first, then all of us took a step back---except Jonathan.

"Um, I'm confused." Jonathan scratched his head. "How come it looks like there's *raw hamburger* coming out of the pumpkin?"

"Jonathan, *please*, just *back away* from him," I pleaded, my voice shaking.

The pumpkin wasn't next to the guy's head.

The pumpkin *was* his head.

And what looked like hamburger, was his *brains*.

As soon as that fact registered in Jonathan's skull, he shrieked and stumbled backwards, falling on his butt. He scooted away from the body. Kurt dry-heaved and covered his mouth.

"How--how--?!" Jonathan stammered.

"I don't know, but this shit's *serious*. Someone's screwing around with some *really* dark magic."

We watched as a girl dressed as Little Red Riding Hood was being chased by a wolf-man. She grabbed a trashcan in mid-run and knocked it over, hoping to slow his pursuit. It did no good. He jumped right over it. The wolf-man was wearing blue jeans, a red lumberjack shirt and sneakers, but his head was a perverted, hideous, dog-face. He also sported furry hands. Snarling, snapping, and drooling, he continued to chase after the girl with a limp-run. I held an arm out, sending my energies after him, forcing him to stop in his tracks. I suspended him in mid-air a foot above ground. He thrashed and clawed at his surroundings, confused. The guys ran over to the girl while I stayed put on the sidewalk behind a tree, out of sight.

"You okay?" Jonathan asked her.

"What's *wrong* with him?! What's wrong with my *boyfriend*?!" She yelled at them, wrapping the cape around herself.

Kurt put his hands on his hips again. "That *thing* is your boyfriend?"

"Yes! He was wearing a mask! But then, it looked like it started to *melt* into his face! He couldn't get it off! Then--" She broke down crying, still hysterical. Kurt had to shake her to make her focus.

"Just get to the police and tell them what happened. *Go*!"

Still dazed and bewildered, she took off. I came out of hiding then, still focused on holding the wolf-guy in place.

"So, what are we gonna do with big, bad, Huff-n-Puff?" I asked. "He's still alive, unlike Pumpkin Boy behind us." I glanced back to the sidewalk.

Jonathan picked up a rock and hit him in the head. Wolf-Guy howled in pain and snapped at Jonathan. He stepped back.

"What'd you do *that* for?" I reprimanded.

"I was *trying* to knock him out." He shrugged his shoulders.

Getting a little closer to Wolf-Guy, I could see where the

mask had somehow fused itself to his neck, his head now the mask come-to-life.

"It like a B-movie version of *American Werewolf in London,* except we can call it, *Cheesy Werewolf in Chestnut Hill.*" Kurt quipped with a smirk of annoyance.

"We could tie him down somewhere," Kim suggested, then pointed to a bench. "How about there? We can use strips of Jonathan's cape to tie his hands and feet together."

"Aw, *man*!" Jonathan mumbled, reluctantly taking off his cape to start tearing long pieces of sheeting for us.

Once we got Wolf-Guy situated, we left him squirming and writhing on the public bench. He snarled and barked at us. At least he wouldn't be able to harm anyone, as long as people kept their distance from him.

The sights were getting stranger. Transparent, hideous-looking creatures, skeletal forms of half-decayed bodies, and totally indescribable monsters were floating everywhere. Screams of bloody murder were still permeating the air.

"Are these things *ghosts*?" Kurt asked, holding my arm tight.

"Worse." Kim paused. "They're thought-forms."

"Like, things from out of people's dreams?" I asked.

He nodded. "And from out of their conscious thoughts."

"They won't *hurt* us, will they?" Kurt asked, eyeing the floating grotesques. A single, disembodied eye the size of a basketball eyed him back.

"Being so transparent, I doubt it. Thought forms are only as strong as the amount of energy one puts into creating them."

"So, if we see something really freaky as hell and *solid, then* we need to worry, right?" Jonathan offered.

"You got it," Kim replied. Kurt tried waving off the huge eye, hoping to make it dissipate.

We continued down the middle of the street, the mayhem still surrounding us. Overturned trashcans filled with garbage were scattered about, smashed pumpkins and gourds everywhere---but at least these were *normal* pumpkins, thank goodness---torn Halloween decorations, purple and green streamers and props on the ground, chrysanthemums that were ripped out of people's lawns and strewn around, not to mention toilet paper, candy, and busted eggs that were trampled on in the street before us.

"See! *That's* the shit I'm talking about!" Kurt started his hissy-fit again. "People being all wasteful and stupid--look at all those eggs!" He pointed to the shattered shells on the ground and the yolks on someone's car window. "Folks should be cooking that shit up and eating it for breakfast, not tossing them around for fun!"

More kids and teens were running around like crazy, a lot of them unfortunately bestowed with their newly adopted horror heads. We saw everything from evil clowns, to aliens, to demonic-looking monsters. We even saw some reptilian-like heads and plenty of revolting, nasty skulls. The worst ones seems to be the freakish, 'human face' masks that had extra---or bloody---drooping eyes, hideous, sloppy-looking stitches keeping their 'skin' together, or ones that looked like they were exposing brains, muscle or bone. But now, those people were experiencing the *pain* of having such heads. Their moans and screams were just too much. All of them were trying to pull their masks off to no avail, and a lot of them were gushing *real* blood. Someone sporting a Raptor head was happily chomping down on its ravaged victim.

Kim spotted a little kid trying to get his mask off, and ran towards him. We followed. The kid cried and wailed, more terrified than anything. He tripped and fell, still trying to peel it off.

"Hold on! We'll help you!" Kim said, holding the kid steady. "Kurt, pull the mask up from where it's connecting to his skin."

Kurt whined in protest, but pulled, regardless. As I watched, I flinched every time Kurt yanked at it, because the kid kept on screaming in pain. The mask looked like it was *crazy-glued* to him. It started to shrink and form itself around the kid's head, tightening and suffocating him. He thrashed about in a panic.

"Kurt, c'mon!" Kim exclaimed, the kid wriggling under him in protest.

"I can't! It's too tough!"

I focused my power on separating the mask from the kid's face, and it was working. Kurt managed to roll the mask past the kid's nose, and we could see up to his terror-stricken eyes.

Then, out of nowhere, I was knocked to the ground by some…*thing*. It looked like a cross between a decaying wild boar carcass and a *very* large maggot. I shrieked, losing concentration, and the mask reattached itself to the kid, sealing his fate.

Jonathan grabbed a downed tree branch and whacked the holy hell out of the creature's larval lower-half. Wet, reddish- brown intestines and a pool of bloody, squirming, yellow earthworms exploded from the thing. Jonathan yelped as he got entrails on him, and the boar lunged forward, biting down on the branch, snapping a piece off. Giving a war-cry, Jonathan raised the branch high, slamming it into the thing's head, crushing its skull. The creature now motionless, I crawled away, panting, my heart racing. I felt very woozy, and struggled to keep calm.

"WHAT THE **FUCK** WAS THAT?!" he yelled, smoothing his hair back from his forehead, eyes wide. "Are you okay? What the **HELL** is going on?!"

I took a deep breath. "Your guess is as good as mine. Kurt? Kim? How's the kid?" I asked, as I stood on trembling legs.

They walked up to me, their faces solemn. "Well, the kid now officially looks like Frankenstein's son."

"Shit," I spat. "Where'd he go?"

"He took off. Sorry, Miss C," Kurt answered. "But are *you* alright? What the flyin' rat's ass is ***that***?!" He looked at the thing Jonathan killed.

"This is *definitely* a fully-manifested thought-form," Kim answered, poking the remains with the tree branch. "Holy cow. *Amazing*!" He kept poking at it, simply awed, while Kurt's face was pinched in disgust.

A few worms tried crawling on Kim's shoe, and he stepped on them, grimacing as he heard them pop underfoot.

"What kind of SICK FUCKS think up shit like *that*?!" Jonathan exploded again.

"Well, I know one thing! If I see ***anyone*** dressed up like Michael, Freddy, Jason, Pinhead, or any of those other famous murderin' fucknuts, I'm ***outta*** here!" Kurt exclaimed, his skin glistening in nervousness.

I inhaled deeply. "C'mon guys, we *gotta* keep a level head, and figure out what the hell is happening, and *why*."

We continued our trek down the street, the chaos nonstop. Some cars now had broken windows, as did a few stores. More and more people were lying everywhere, either in pain, or, perish the thought---dead. We saw a growing fire inside of a demolished store, and cop sirens and ambulances were sounding off in the distance.

"Ya know, even though all this doesn't make sense, ya gotta admit, it's kinda *cool*," Jonathan said with a little half-smirk.

"COOL?!" Kurt yelled. "Huge, ugly, nasty-ass pig-maggots and people with gory, monster heads are *not* cool!"

"Something *extremely* malicious is behind this," I stated. "Malicious and flat-out evil."

"But *what*?" Kim asked. "Do you know how many

demons are out there that could be causing this? Not to mention regular, sick, twisted, *people*."

"Like we need any more *Natashas* causing trouble," Kurt mumbled.

Up ahead, we saw a small entourage coming towards us. At least they weren't running amok like everyone else. They must have been just as baffled as we were. We started walking towards them.

"Maybe they might be able to tell us what's going on!" Jonathan said. "Maybe they saw something we haven't yet that could give us some clues."

As they continued to approach us, we could tell something was wrong with them, so we stopped. They were shuffling, stumbling about. Then one of them puked up a reddish-yellow fluid.

Then we heard the groaning.

Kurt froze, his eyes wide in a panic. "Aw, HELLLL no! Fuck *this* shit!" He grabbed my wrist, yanking me in the opposite direction.

"Holy ***crap***! Talk about your George Romero rejects!" Jonathan quipped, following after me and Kurt. Kim was right behind Jonathan, looking pale as a ghost, pardon the pun.

We turned down a dark alley with a wrought-iron, gothic-looking gate. Hopefully, nothing would spot us here. Jonathan burst out in laughter.

"Wow! Is *this* a freakin' trip or *what*?!"

The three of us stared at him hard, and Jonathan sobered up quick, trying to get serious again as he grabbed the gate and lazily swung himself from it.

"Well, shouldn't we at least destroy those things before they wind up eating other people?" Jonathan asked me. "I wouldn't mind playing baseball with a head or two." He gestured like he was holding a bat, and swung it. "Right off their necks with a ***thwock***!"

"The thing is---what if they're *already* people, *dressed up* like zombies? We *don't* want to kill anyone." I rubbed my temples.

"Not being able to tell if they're the real deal or not makes it hard," Kim added.

"As long as we're *away* from them, I don't give a shit if we 'thwock' their heads off or not. I *refuse* to have some puking, shamblin', rotten fuckers trying to chow down on my ass!" Kurt peeked around the corner of the building.

Jonathan spotted a kid's candy bag on the ground, long deserted. He grabbed it, quickly checked to see if the loot was good, and then we continued walking.

"Aw, c'mon, Jonathan," I said, disbelieving of his actions, despite the carnage going on.

"Hey, I'm going by the pirate rule!" He grinned, moving his skull aside so he could stuff the new black and orange-colored bag into his.

"What pirate rule?"

"Um, 'take what you can, and give nothing back'…or something like that."

"Okay Purplehead the Pirate, any bright ideas on what to do *next*?" Kurt nervously wrung his shirt.

Jonathan shrugged his shoulders. "How should I know? It's not like we know what started all this crap."

"That's easy! The culprit's been with you *all along*," an

unfamiliar voice spoke. We jumped in surprise and looked around us.

"Disembodied voices… *not* cool," Kurt said. I could feel his heart racing again.

"Where are you?" I asked sternly. "We can't see you. Show yourself!"

"Look up!"

We did, and spotted a little man sitting in a tree, dangling his feet from the branch he sat on. He jumped down from fifteen feet with ease, wearing a white suit, matching shoes and fedora, and stood about three feet tall, with jet black hair and an olive complexion. He also sported a goatee and had cherubic features…

And the eyes of a goat.

"Yeesh," I said to myself, taking a step back. I'd always thought goats' eyes looked weird. They and their respective relatives were the only critters that I knew of that had rectangular-shaped pupils. He radiated a very nasty energy, but not nearly as strong as mine. After that little shock, I regained my composure.

He sized me up. "Lady Abraxas. It's nice to meet you…almost." He snickered.

I frowned. "You're not funny."

"Never said I was," he said nonchalantly, sizing up the guys next. "Your entourage, I assume?"

"They're my *family*, not groupies," I snapped.

Mockingly, he put his chubby hands to his mouth. "Oops. *My bad.* Well then, did you figure out what started all of this?" He gestured out into the street.

"You mean 'who'. You said the culprit was among us," Kurt interrupted, his voice having dropped a couple notches.

"Well, it's more like a 'what' *and* a 'who'." He grinned at us, scratching his ass.

Kurt turned to Jonathan and stared at the pendant. "Aw,

man!”

“Give the young man a cookie!” The goat man mockingly clapped his hands.

“You wished everyday could be Halloween!” I told Jonathan. All the color drained from his face, making him paler than his makeup did. He swallowed, regaining composure.

“Well, I take it back! I ***undo*** it!” He yelled at the demon.

Goat-Man snorted and waved off Jonathan before he folded his chubby arms. “*Please*. Like I’d make it *that* easy for you.” He rolled his eyes at us. “You people are *so* easy to mess with, it’s ridiculous! Remember what happened to your precious *Lord*, My Lady? Nice job you all did wiping my fellow brother out, by the way.” He sneered at us.

“Shut up,” I hissed, and he grinned that ugly, little grin of his. “We’re *not* average people, as you well know.”

“But the fact remains---you once *were*. Still prone to human emotions, wants and desires. That’ll *never* change!” He smiled again. Boy, did he have some really big, annoying-looking, horse teeth. “We make you love the stupid things, and disregard what’s most important. So *gullible…!*” His voice trailed off, going off on his own little tangent, not talking to us directly.

“Look, *I take it all back*!” Jonathan pleaded. “People are getting really fucked up out there!”

“What’s said is said,” Goat-Man replied, sounding bored. “I knew you’d be a *perfect* candidate for my gift---with your fractured mentality and all…”

“You put that pendant on the ground for him to *find*?!” I yelled, balling my fists up.

“Of course! What a fun way to bring Hell here on earth, at least, a *small* part of it.” He chuckled again, and it was getting on my nerves.

“But I thought demons didn’t bother messing with other people on this night!” Jonathan said, sounding defeated.

"And who made *that* bullshit up?" Goat-Man retorted. "Well, *some* of us don't *have* to work, but that doesn't stop the majority of us from fucking with the idiots out there who like to 'summon' us for kicks. Halloween is *not* our little holiday off from screwing with you all. We're always busy. Always busy…" He snorted, and hocked a lump of light-green phlegm onto the sidewalk. "And *I* still have a quota to fill before the year is out." He strode up to Jonathan and looked up at him, fearless, then glanced at us. "You don't get it! Golden Boy here is my ticket to *Easy Street*! With his unlimited imagination, frustrations, grudges and determination, the world can be at my fingertips in a matter of hours, *minutes* even! I won't have to lift a finger to do shit for the Bossman ever again! Hell, I could even ***be*** the new Bossman!" He paused, in thought. "Oooo, *me*, the ***new*** Bossman! The sound of that makes me wanna *squirt*." He rubbed his grimy, little hands together in glee at the idea.

I grimaced, trying hard not to imagine exactly what it was that he 'squirted', and from what orifice it came from. The guys stood there, dumbfounded for a moment.

"So… you're *using* Jonathan to do your dirty work!" Kim blurted out.

"And another cookie for the gentleman to my left!" Goat-Man clapped again, and he started reminding me of either a used car salesman, or a slapstick, game show host. I couldn't decide which persona fitted him better, but either one would still be annoying.

Kurt was fuming. "You simple-assed, son of a--"

"Na-ah! Naughty, naughty!" he said, holding a dirt-encrusted finger to his lips. The fingernail was thick and pointed. "*Shhhh*!"

Kurt made a muffled noise. We looked at him, and saw he had *no mouth*. The remaining three of us screamed in unison.

I turned and looked at the goat man, my eyes a solid

black. I reached out and gripped him by his collar, picking him up. "**Stop it**. *Now*!"

Goat-Man yelped in surprise and waved his hand at Kurt. When we heard Kurt shriek, I was never more happy to hear that sound. I looked at the demon again.

"Stop this bullshit, and undo what was done!"

"Gotta catch me first," he replied, snapping his fingers, and he was gone in a cloud of smoke. Nothing was left but the clothes he wore and the smell of sulfur in the air.

"Oh, this is ridiculous!" I snapped, tossing his suit jacket aside. It slapped against a bench, dropping to the ground. "Just fan*fucking*tastic!"

"Now we gotta *find* that little goat bastard?!" Kurt yelled to the sky. "Can we say, 'needle in a haystack'?!"

"If we don't, it'll still be Halloween tomorrow, and the day after that, until we *do*," I replied. "We're gonna need Kiera's help."

2

"You think this situation is contained in just this area?" Jonathan asked me while we cautiously made our way back down the street. Two normal looking girls were being chased by someone with a overly-large alien head, and another with a head that looked like it was half eaten away by acid. I concentrated on them, then made a motion like I was shoving them far away from the girls. They went sailing backwards, one of them landing on the hood of someone's car, the other tossed through a store window that was already broken. Confused as to how that happened, they took off, unharmed.

"Well, I sure as hell *hope* so," I answered, watching black and purple paper bats fly after a screaming, little boy. A barrage of scampering rubber rats weren't too far behind. "If this insanity is all over the city, I can't even *begin* to imagine the amount of chaos going on."

"Maybe it just depends on how strong your wish was," Kim suggested to Jonathan.

"Speaking of that, no more wishes for *you*!" Kurt took the pendant off Jonathan's neck. "We don't need any *more* weird shit going on tonight."

"Aw, you can't blame Jonathan completely, Kurt," I said, watching some kid's spilled gummy worms and gummy bugs crawling their way up the street. "*None* of us suspected something as crazy as *this* would happen."

Kim got the crap scared out of him next when an eyeless, emaciated, spectral form with long, straight black hair floated alongside him for a moment, before passing us. Kurt shivered.

"Things with no eyes seriously creep me out," he said. "That's almost right up there with *zombies*."

"And speaking of zombies," Jonathan interrupted,

pointing ahead of us. "*They* haven't really gone anywhere, yet."

Kurt gave a tiny, high-pitched noise.

The zombies were looking in trashcans, taking things out and eating them. Two of them had wandered over to the dead, pumpkin-headed guy, squatted down, and began scooping out the bloody, clumpy remains of his head with their hands. Without hesitation, they ate it. I clutched my stomach and felt it churn as Jonathan covered his mouth. Kurt belched as if he were about to spew, while Kim lost the last of the candy he ate right onto the sidewalk.

Jonathan took a closer look at the zombies on parade.

"That one looks like the kid that was toilet-papering the tree earlier!" He pointed to one that was mindlessly walking around in front of a building.

"So that confirms they're *people* and not real, living-dead," Kim said, looking a little green around the gills. "I don't know if I could deal with real ones right now."

"Same here!" Kurt quickly added.

I sent a mental message to Kiera about what was happening. Ryan was in Harrisburg, PA for a few days on a business trip, so I didn't want to tell him and have him worry. But still, I wondered how things were up in that neck of the woods. Harrisburg was only a two hour drive from where we lived.

"Miss C! You're okay!" came Kiera's shrill voice in my head.

"Thank God," I said out loud. "Are you still at your party?"

"Heck, no! I got the hell outta there! Everyone's becoming what they're dressed up as! This crap looks like something from out of a low-budget, horror movie!" She paused, taking a quick breather. *"Where are you?"*

"Chestnut Hill, roaming around Germantown Ave. Um, Kiera, something *really* goofy happened while we were out."

*"Goofy is an **understatement**! I had an actual skeleton ask me for change so he could call home to find out if his mom was alright! Can you **imagine** how insane that looked?!"*

I sighed and told her no, then gave her the rundown on what happened on our trick-or-treating trip. She said *a lot* of 'Oh my Gods' before I was done.

"Okay, the goat guy scares me a bit," she said. *"But the trouble will be in finding out the demon's name, and how he can be vanquished, **plus** finding out how to reverse the stuff Jonathan did."* She paused. *"He really had goat's eyes? Ew."*

"I'm glad I'm not the only one creeped out by that."

"I'll head home and get started on research."

"We'll meet you there," I said out loud. "We're not staying out here a minute longer."

Jonathan pouted.

"Wipe that look off your face, boy!" Kurt yelled. "All this *bullshit* is *your* fault."

"See you soon, then," Kiera continued. *"Be careful."*

"We will," I replied, then looked at the guys. "Alrighty, let's try to get home in one piece."

"Sans zombies?" Kurt asked sweetly.

"You're right. Let's go a different way."

"Let's all hold hands and teleport!" Jonathan said excitedly.

"Hell, no. I haven't quite perfected that trick. I usually don't wind up *exactly* where I want to be, despite it being close to my destination. I experienced *that* one too many times trying to get to Kurt and Kiera during the Natasha fiasco. Plus, it's pretty draining."

"Say no more," Kurt replied, closing his eyes. In seconds, a cab pulled up alongside the curb.

"You summoned a cabbie?" I asked.

"Nope. *Wished* for it." Kurt grinned, dangling the pendant from his fingers.

"*Kurt*!" I reprimanded.

"At least I used a wish *sensibly*." He eyed Jonathan, and Jonathan threw his hands up in response.

"Dude! How was I supposed to know this would happen?! Gimmie a break!"

"Not until all this goes away, *Grimace*." Kurt glanced at his hideous, purple hair as we got into the cab.

"Ya know, I've *always* wondered why Ronald McDonald called that purple thing Grimace," Jonathan started. "I mean, a 'grimace' is a *frown*, right? Isn't Ronald and the gang supposed to be all *cheerful*?"

We groaned in reply.

We arrived at the mansion without any problems on the way, but once we stepped out of the cab, it was a different story altogether.

One jerk dressed up as a lame-assed, 'traditional' Dracula was sucking on a girl's neck. He saw us, raised his black cape in the air, and hissed. The girl's body had dropped to the ground with a dull *thud,* her limbs askew.

Kurt leaned towards Kim and said, "I'm almost impressed." Kim snorted.

Dracula-Dude came for me next. I folded my arms, looking bored. He couldn't be serious! He hissed at me, and I rolled my eyes. I *really* didn't have time for his bullshit.

"Oh, *shut up*!" I snapped. He stopped and blinked, taken aback by my reaction. "Take a nap!" Sounding blasé, I pushed his forehead with the tip of my index finger. He dropped to the ground like a rag doll, snoring. Jonathan laughed at him.

"That was *cool*, Christine!"

Another guy came crawling towards us on the sidewalk, moaning in agony. Kim looked at us.

"Should we help?"

"The thing is, will we be *able* to," I muttered. Making

my way towards the guy, they followed me.

I started to wonder if he was wearing a mask at all. His face looked like it was ripped clean off. I could see part of his bloody, wet skull through what appeared to be half-chewed muscle on one side of his face. One of his eyes was missing, the other rolling around in its socket, unfocused. His tongue still remained in his head, his teeth also bloodied. His hands were dirty, raw, and scratched up badly, knuckles worn to the bone.

"Help *meeeee….*" His voice sounded hollow and distant. He reached out for us, grabbed the hem of Jonathan's jeans, then let go, having passed out…or died.

Another guy came stumbling up the street. He sported a pumpkin head too, but he looked like he was trying to hold it together. He screamed, bloody pumpkin seeds and a dark-red, thick liquid oozing down his carved eyes, nose, and mouth. One half of his head had already caved in. He simply passed by us as if we weren't even there, the horrid smell of rotting pumpkin and decaying meat making us gag. My stomach lurched.

"House…*now*." I said, and we made a mad dash to the mansion. We got in, and I slammed the door behind myself, leaning against it. Sighing, we relished the quiet normalcy of the foyer, thankful to be home.

I looked at Jonathan more closely, his bedraggled, black bed sheet in tatters after dealing with the wolf-guy incident, his bag of candy attached to his belt, with his skull inside, sitting on top of his loot. His purple hair was sticking up in all sorts of crazy angles, with remnants of dried pig-maggot blood on his jeans and shirt.

He looked hideous *and* hilarious.

I stared at Jonathan harder, leaning towards him.

"You have a little maggot stuck in your hair." I pointed at it.

He yelped, slapping at his messy coif until he knocked the white, squirming larva to the floor.

Kurt noticed my mouth slowly curl into a grin, and that's what made him suddenly burst out in laughter. Kim, holding his sides, plopped himself on the third step, tears rolling down his face. Then Jonathan and I chimed in. It was the best way to release all that tension of what we just went through.

Kiera rushed out of the tea room. "Guys!" she said happily, hugging all of us. "I'm *sooo* glad you made it home safely!" She got a better look at Jonathan, and wrinkled her nose at him. "What the *hell* were you supposed to be?! *The Joker*'s cousin?"

"Nothing, really. Just *not me*." He shrugged.

"Find anything?" I asked her.

"Not yet. I'm still researching." She sighed. "With no name to go by, this isn't easy."

"Oh my God, Kiera, you missed it!" Jonathan clutched his goody bag, grinning.

"Missed what?"

"What happened *outside*!" His grin grew wider.

"Just now?"

"Yeah! Christine put Dracula to sleep, and this dude walked by with a rotten pumpkin head! And earlier, we saw one with his head already bashed in, brains and all!"

"*Too many* pumpkin heads in one night, if you ask *me*," Kurt grumbled.

"And there was this dude on the sidewalk with a meaty lookin' skull head! He grabbed my pant leg, and just…keeled over. Man, this whole night is *whacked*!"

Jonathan *sounded* upset, but his smile proved otherwise. He was really reveling in tonight. He didn't shy away or keep quiet or look nervous *once* while we were out there. On any normal day, he was all of that, and sometimes *worse*.

Right now, he was *truly* in his element.

October really *was* the only time when he could feel comfortable in his own skin. I was seeing the proof for myself.

"And…you're *happy* about all of this?" Kiera frowned, put a hand on her hip, and raised an eyebrow at him.

His chipper vibe dropped like brick.

I cleared my throat and put an arm around Jonathan. "We'll join you guys in a sec. Keep researching until we get back."

"Absolutely, Miss C," Kurt said as he and Kim bowed at me and walked with Kiera to the den. I led Jonathan to the tea room, his candy bag bopping his leg as he walked. We sat on the couch and I looked at him for a moment.

"You really *do* want it to be Halloween every day, don't you?"

He looked down, and sighed.

"Spill it, kiddo. You know you want to."

He looked at me, giving me a expression that was near tears.

"If you had to grow up with a alcoholic mom, shitheel dad, and deal with a bunch of dickheads who'd tease you about it daily, you'd want things to be *way* different too, wouldn't you?"

"Of course, but--"

"I tried to make friends, honest. But none really stuck, ya know? I had no 'best' friend. People just naturally kept their distance, or didn't care. Either way, I was always *alone*."

I put my hand on top of his. "Jonathan, although I didn't have the kind of parents you did, I was *still* in the same boat as you."

His eyes expressed a light of hope that *someone* might understand what he was feeling.

"When I was your age, even *younger*, I was thinking and dreaming the *same* things you are now. I wanted to live in a different place, an alternate world where things would go my way. And on my really, *really* bad days, I used to wish I had a different family, too. I seriously believed I was switched at birth." I snorted, remembering those days. "School kids were nothing more then people I had to tolerate. I was teased and talked about every day. No one dared to fight me, though. I think I had that 'look' that said I'd murder them if they tried." I chuckled to myself, and Jonathan watched me, really into my story. "Once they saw my--*reactions*--when they went too far, they *really* left me alone, then." I sighed. "I was *rarely* a happy camper, trust me. I *always* felt like I was on the outside, looking in."

Immediately, the connection I had with Jonathan became stronger. It was like his energies reached out and grabbed a tighter hold to mine.

"So you can see why I *like* things the way they are, right? Minus the people dying out there, of course."

"But that's just it, Jonathan! This wish of yours is making innocent people *die*."

"It's not like I *want* people to die, Christine! But, I *can* wish for folks not to get hurt or killed. *That* might put a bit of a crimp in that goat dude's plans, right?"

"That's a start, but, *still*--"

"I thought you'd *understand* Christine! I don't *fit* in a normal world…if you can call it *normal* to begin with. But now that I have a chance to change things, I'll *force* the world to fit into mine. I'll *make* it work, I promise!"

"That's a dangerous idea, kiddo. There's no quick-fast way to change *anything*. Things take *time*. You'd rather mess with the natural order of things?"

"The natural order is *un*natural! It *sucks*! What's the point in having the powers we have if we can't change things to our liking?"

"We *can*, but it has to be done *when needed*, and *subtly*.

We can't scare the masses. People can act like herds of mad, crazy cattle when in a panic."

"But I'm *glad* the goat man picked me. I can take this magic of his and change things for the better!"

"By making every day *Halloween*?"

He paused.

"*Their* kind of magic *always* comes with a price! You can't make deals with the devil, *or* his flunkies! It just like *The Monkey's Paw*…only a zillion times worse! Besides," I raised my eyebrow. "Why let yourself be a flunky ***to*** a flunky?"

He stopped short. "Whoa, you're right, Christine," he said softly. "I'm sorry."

"Awww," I reached over and gave him a hug. "It's alright. And know what? I'll help you get over this *thing* you have, once this mess is over with. Promise."

He hugged me tighter. "Thank you, Christine."

"So, let's go find the gang and tell Kurt about that new wish to stop people from dying. I'm sure he'll give the pendant back to you for *that*."

We got up, and raced out of the tea room.

3

"Six eyes are better than two!" Kiera said happily when we entered the den. "We found him in my trusty book of angels and demons!" She held up a large, hardback book and pointed to a picture of a portly, little demon that stood upright on one fat, elephant-looking leg, with sharp teeth, a certain, extra-long male appendage--which gave new meaning to the phrase, 'kick stand'--small bat-like wings that wouldn't be strong enough to carry its weight, extra big, pointed, elven-like ears, four arms with eagle talons on its hands, and those unmistakable goat eyes. I doubted I'd want to touch him again after seeing that image of him in true form.

"Its name is Ock," she started. "Not to be confused with O-c-*h*, an angel of the sun. Ock is 'cousin' to Af."

"They must've started running out of ideas for names *down there*," Kurt quipped.

"Who the hell is Af?" Jonathan asked.

"And what's Ock's specialties?" I asked her.

"Well, Af is a 'prince of wrath', an angel of destruction, ruler over the death of humans."

I shuddered, assuming Abraxas' powers must override Af's final decisions when it came to things like that, as I remembered the very first battle Ryan and I fought together. She continued. "Ock is a lower demon, more like a trickster, and very mischievous. He's not physically violent, as he prefers to offer his magic to humans so he can basically watch us fuck ourselves up with it."

Kurt dangled the pendant again, as if reminding us.

"In other words, he doesn't like getting his own hands dirty," I said, and Kiera nodded.

"Did you know there's even an angel called Aha?" Kim mentioned out loud. "Very interesting."

"Did you find a way to vanquish him, or at least reverse the damage from the magic that's set loose?" I plopped myself into a chair.

Kiera sighed. "This is gonna sound *really* retarded, but, if we can trap him somehow, get him in the middle of an open field at high noon, while covered in holy water, hyssop, and lilacs, *and* hold a mirror in front of him, we should be able to send him back, undoing all his magic. As long as he's roaming around scott-free on earth, his powers only gets more stronger."

"Run that by me *again*?" Kurt squinted an eye at her. "We gotta do *what* to him?"

Kiera sighed in impatience. "Put it this way, Kurt. Ock is a petty demon, not all that powerful. Therefore, his banishing technique might seem silly to you."

"Silly's an *understatement,* girl."

"Trust me, I've heard *stranger*." She shuddered, as if rcmcmbcring somcthing. "So bc *glad*, Kurt. Usually, thc stronger a demon is, the *harder* it can be to banish him, and the techniques even *more* complicated to do."

"Okay, okay, I got it." Kurt rolled his eyes. "This goofy-ass shit," he said and sighed. "So douse him with some water and flowers and force him to look at himself in a mirror." He paused. "A *mirror*?"

"It'll probably reflect his true self, and most of them don't like to see their own reflections. Allegedly, their own images frighten even *themselves*, so I guess revealing his true form will scare him right back to Hell."

Kurt looked at the picture of Ock in the book.

"Humph! If I was him and lookin' like *that*, I wouldn't want to see myself *either*!"

4

"At this point, I'm afraid to even *look* at the news," I said to them. Kim nodded at me in agreement.

"But we *need* to," Kurt suggested. "So we can at least see how far this craziness is spreading."

Kiera sighed and got up. She walked over to the television that was sitting in the corner of the room, and turned it on.

"Police are baffled as to why citizens are running amok over certain areas of Germantown and Chestnut Hill. Some are suggesting that this might be a case of biological warfare, while religious fanatics are claiming that this is a sign of the end times. Further investigation continues as some people have been rounded up and taken into custody, and oddly, all of them seem to lack comprehension skills."

We watched as the anchorwoman spoke to the camera, the background being part of the jail she was doing her report in. Behind bars was the wolf guy we left tied up on the bench, who was now sporting a muzzle, a few psychotic clowns that climbed the bars and made lewd, obscene gestures behind her back, and some guy dressed like the Grim Reaper. Ironically, Grim Reaper Guy reached out and touched a clown, who dropped to the cell floor with a *thud.*

"Shit. Kurt, give the pendant back to Jonathan, quick," I said, still staring at the TV screen.

"Are you *nuts*, Miss C?!" he replied, eyes wide.

"At least let him wish not for any more people to die. Did you see what the Grim Reaper just did?"

Kurt smirked, but gave the skeleton key to Jonathan, who closed his eyes, making his wish. Then, very obediently, he handed it back to Kurt.

"Thanks," Kurt said, putting it back in his pocket.

"For everyone at home, it's strongly advised that you *do not* open your doors to anyone, and keep everyone inside until further announcements are made," the anchorwoman continued.

"Well, so far, so good, if you wanna call this 'good'," Kiera said. "It sounds like it's only in this area for now."

"So, the sooner we grab that goat-bastard, the better." Kurt smirked.

Then, something odd happened. I watched as the dead psycho clown slowly *stood up*. My heart felt like ice, and squeezed.

"Guys…are you still watching?"

"Clown Dude just got up!" Kim said, gawking at the screen. "But…*how*? He was already dead *before* Jonathan made his wish!"

I paused. "Jonathan, how *exactly* did you word it?" I started wringing my hands in nervousness.

"I---I just said I didn't want anyone to die! There's no way Ock could mess with *that*, right?"

I looked off to my side. "Actually, when you think about it… yeah, *he can*. The wish wasn't exactly *to the point*. It still gives him *a lot* of leeway to screw it up and twist it to *his* liking."

"Aw, *c'mon*!" Jonathan yelled to the ceiling, wishing it was Ock. "You *asshole*! I wish ***you*** were fucking dead!"

Kiera looked panicked. "So, since Jonathan wished for no one to die, do you think that'll mean…?"

"Probably anyone who's dead, will come back to life," Kurt concluded. "And if someone *does* get killed, *they'll* still come back to life, too." He began to tremble. "This is like my *worst* nightmare come true! Zombies, zombies, *everywhere*, and not *one* gun to shoot 'em with!" He balled himself up on the couch, holding a pillow to his chest.

"There's *got* to be a way to outsmart Ock with his own

trinket!" I said. "But in the meantime, we need to start gathering what we need to vanquish him." I looked at Kiera. "Are there any flower shops around here? That way, we can grab hyssop and lilacs."

"I'll have to check. Let me get the phone book," she replied, leaving the den.

"Now…where can we get holy water?" I said to myself.

"That church on Germantown Ave.," Kim mentioned. "We passed it on the way back home. You think it might have some?"

"It's worth a shot," I said. "But that means we have to go back out."

"Can I sit this one out, Miss C?" Kurt whined. "*Pleeeeease*?"

I exhaled through my nose. He sighed and got up.

"Kurt, it's not like they'll *get you*. Only if you *allow* them to." I gave him a knowing look.

"I know *that,* but, I just…don't…like… ***zombies***!"

I sighed, and sent Kiera a mental note that we were going to a church that Kim spotted earlier, and would be right back once we got the holy water. She sounded tense as she said to hurry back home.

As the four of us were about to leave, we ran right into Dino and Dennis, their eyes wide in terror. Dino had a bloody hand print smeared across his right shoulder, and Dennis had assorted splotches of red all over his clean, white shirt, jacket, and jeans.

"Christine! Don't go out there!" Dennis exclaimed. "Everyone's a *monster*!" He wrapped his arms around my waist and squeezed me tight. I patted his back, trying to comfort him.

"Screw this shit," Dino snapped. "I ain't leaving the house until *that*--" He pointed outside. "--Goes the hell away!" He pulled on his clothes, showing them to me. "Look what some dead-ass fucker did to my shirt!"

"It's okay, guys. We know what's gong on. Go help Kiera. She's probably in the kitchen, looking through the phone book. She'll explain everything to you."

"Gotcha," Dino said, and Dennis followed after him. "I ***hate*** Halloween!" Dino yelled out, and I knew he meant that expressly for Jonathan, who flinched in reply.

Once outside, I took a deep breath. "Okay, Kim. Lead the way."

We made it back to Germantown Ave., still hearing a scream on occasion. It wasn't as much mayhem as earlier. Probably people were getting smart and running back to their homes. As for everyone else tainted by the wish, *that* was a different story.

Cop cars were going up and down the streets, trying to capture the bad crowds, and having a hell of a time trying. We decided to stay in the shadows. Although the cops were doing their best to keep the crazy characters at bay, they really wouldn't be a help to *us* if they interfered in our own plans.

When we got to the church, I looked at it and sighed.

"Kim, sweetie, usually Catholic churches have holy water, and this one isn't Catholic."

Kim looked despondent. "Aw man, are you *sure*? It won't hurt to check, right?"

"Well, okay, but we'd better make it quick."

We ran behind the church, away from the glaring spotlights on it. I used my powers to unlock one of the back doors, envisioning the little pins in the tumbler shifting around until I heard the click, signaling it was open. We tiptoed inside.

And like I guessed, no holy water anywhere. I groaned in frustration.

"Sorry, Christine." Kim sounded despondent.

"It's alright. You tried." I gave him a smile. "But there's still plenty of churches around. We just gotta find the right one."

As soon as I locked the door, a glaring white light suddenly flashed on the four of us, preventing us from seeing.

Cops. I sneered in annoyance.

"Hold it right there!" we heard one of them say. "You're under arrest for trespassing and vandalism!"

"We ain't vandalize *shit*!" Kurt yelled at them. "We even locked the damn door!"

"*Kurt*!" I said, yanking his arm, getting him to follow me. Jonathan and Kim raced after us as we made a mad dash across the church's front lawn and across the street, with me praying the cops wouldn't open fire on us anyway. Once we were behind a building, I heard the cops yelling after us as I told everyone to hold hands. Thinking fast, I made us teleport to another section of Germantown Ave. We landed in a different cemetery from the one Jonathan was in earlier that night. Each of us was scattered throughout different sections of the churchyard, dizzy, but unharmed.

"Sheesh! Now I see why you don't want to teleport much." Kurt brushed the dead grass off his pants as he walked towards me. Kim sat up and shook his head. Jonathan was holding his own head, stumbling slightly.

"I feel queasy," he said, holding his stomach. "Ugh. Teleporting sucks! I thought it'd be cool."

"Maybe the more you practice, the easier it'll get," I assumed. "But still, it's not my favorite way to travel, unless in a dire emergency."

"Okay, so where are we, exactly?" Kurt asked me.

I held a finger to my lips and pointed up the sidewalk. Three psycho clowns had gotten into a brawl for whatever reason, kicking, hitting, spitting, and throwing garbage, rotten pumpkins and gourds at each other. One grabbed a trick-or-treat bag off the ground and covered another's head, trying to suffocate the other with it. A lone, tainted person that turned into who-knew-what was shuffling his way across the street, ignoring them. We watched him until he was a good distance away from us, not wanting to draw any unnecessary attention to ourselves.

"Although this church isn't a Catholic one, that one ***is***." I pointed further down the block. "So let's get there as fast as we can."

As we weaved through the grave markers, I got the strangest feeling that the ground was trembling. I brushed it off at first, blaming my nervousness. We straddled the fencing around the churchyard, and made our way down the street, dead bodies scattered everywhere like broken dolls. Once we snuck into the church, we looked around as quickly as we could. Usually basins of holy water were at the entrances, but we didn't see any.

"Maybe around the pulpit area?" Kim suggested, and we raced down the middle isle between the pews.

Thank the stars, a basin was there. It seemed to glow in the light, the answer to our problems. But suddenly, I looked at the guys, flustered again.

"Oh, for cryin' out loud! Does anyone have anything we can put the water *in*?"

"Aw, *damn*!" Kurt slapped his forehead in response our thoughtlessness.

Without a word, Jonathan raced back out of the church. I knew he went hunting to find something.

I sat on a pew, taking in my surroundings, catching a breather. So peaceful in here, like nothing was going on outside its walls.

If only!

Kurt walked around a bit, admiring the altars and statues until Jonathan tore down the isle, something small in his hand. He handed it to me.

A soda can.

"It was the closest thing I spotted," he said, out of breath.

"It's what's *in* the can that'll count," I replied. "Thank you, sweetie."

I walked up to the basin, and carefully filled the can with water. We made our way back up the isle, and I locked the door behind us.

Back outside, we checked the streets for more cop cars--just in case.

"Coast is clear," I whispered, and we started our fast trek back to the house.

I could still feel rumbling under my feet, and this time, I couldn't ignore it. I frowned, and Kurt also looked at me with the same expression.

"You feel it too, huh?" he asked me.

"Yeah. What the hell *is* that?"

Jonathan stopped, trying to feel what we were talking about. "Oh my God, the ground's moving! It's a fuckin' ***earthquake***!"

"Shh! *Please*, Jonathan! We're doing good so far with things *not* coming after us. Let's keep it that way."

"But he's right, though! It *does* feel like a tiny earthquake." Kim looked at the ground, eyes wide.

As we passed the churchyard we had teleported to, I nearly wanted to pass out.

The soil in the yard was *moving*.

We all stood there like dummies, just gawking at the land, unable to move or take our eyes off the scene.

The ground was pulsing, shifting, like things were

underneath, trying to push their way out. The thin markers began toppling over one by one, then two and three at a time.

Next, the unimaginable happened. Bony hands protruded from the ground like putrid, dead flowers, then came dirty, skeletal *heads*. It was like watching a typical horror movie…except this was *really* happening.

Kurt suddenly let out the biggest, loudest, longest, *girlie-est* shriek I had ever heard in my *life.* He actually scared the shit out me, Kim, *and* Jonathan, more than the things that were coming out of the ground. I yanked on a handful of Kurt's thin dreadlocks to bring him back into focus.

"**THEY'RE ALIVE!**" He started spazzing-out, as if I didn't do a thing to him.

I yanked on his hair a little harder.

"*Owww*!" This time he *did* focus, and Kurt held his dreads away from me. "That shit hurt!"

"C'mon, back to the house! *Hurry*!"

We all made a mad dash up the street.

"Oh my God… oh my God... oh my God…" Kurt chanted to himself, pumping his arms and legs furiously, running with his eyes nearly *closed.* Don't ask me how he was doing that, while *not* tripping on anything.

"All I need *now* is to hear is MJ's famous *Thriller* song, God rest his soul---and if I catch ***any*** zombies in the middle of the street doing some fuckin' synchronized *dance moves*, I'll just curl up and ***die***!"

Jonathan stopped running and laughed so hard, he dropped to his knees, coughing, as tears rolled down his cheeks. Kim tried dragging him while he was still on the ground, to no avail.

"Jonathan! *Get up*," I snapped. He did his best to calm himself, and slowly stood, wheezing, holding his chest.

"***Jesus***!" Kim yelled, staring ahead of us.

Kurt's nightmare just came true.

Although they weren't dancing, they *were* walking haphazardly through the deserted streets, empty, hollow, dirty husks. Tattered, thin, yellowed material hung from dried, blackened bones, and those that were only buried for a few weeks or more were causing a stench that made me heave. I watched as a recently dead body walked towards us, its skin pasty white and swollen, sloughing off in large patches. It opened its eyes, only to have both marbles--or whatever it was that morticians used to fill the eyelids--slide out of its wet, muddy sockets and bounce along the pavement a couple of times before rolling away and dropping though a sewer grate with a *plink*.

Kurt's eyes rolled up into his head, and he dropped to the ground like a puppet that got its strings cut.

I started dragging Kurt out of the street. Kim and Jonathan helped me. We hid behind another building once again, spreading Kurt on the grass.

In the distance, the cops screamed, as their guns fired off. It sounded like they were fast becoming acquainted with the undead.

On the ground, I lightly slapped Kurt's cheeks, pleading for him to wake up. I thought about sending a little jolt of energy through his system, until Jonathan plopped himself beside Kurt's head, gave me a big grin, paused for a moment, then released a long, wet-sounding, massive, *fart*.

"*Ew*, dude! *Five seconds*?!" Kim exclaimed, holding his nose and fanning the air. Jonathan put his finger to his lips.

"Just wait," he whispered to Kim.

I had to jump up and stand back, myself. Sometimes, I wondered what the hell kind of junk that kid ate sometimes.

It took a moment, but Kurt gagged, rolling away from Jonathan before he spoke. "**Jeeesus, Mary, and *Joseph***! What the ***HELL*** you got cloggin' up your colon, boy?! A rotten cheeseburger and onion rings from ***last year***?!"

Jonathan fell on his back in laughter once more, forcing out one last small 'bomb'.

"You don't need smelling salts when you've got *Jonathan* around," Kim quipped.

"What happened?!" Kurt asked me.

"You fainted because you had no desire to see a *Thriller* remake."

He grabbed my arms. "We saw…you mean…I *did* see real, live, *zombies*?"

"Zombies aren't 'live'," Jonathan said dryly.

"You know what I mean!" Kurt snapped. "And *don't* think I'm gonna let that fart thing slide by, *either*!"

"But you were passed out, cold!"

"You could have woke me up *any other* way but ***that way***!" Kurt sniffed the air. "Now the smell's *stuck* on me! *Yeeack*!"

Kim slapped his hand over his mouth to prevent himself from laughing.

"Let's keep walking. It'll go away soon," I said, patting Kurt's back. I bit my tongue hard to keep myself from laughing, too.

But, despite all the sudden silliness, however, I couldn't *wait* to get home. I was tired of the insanity, and I could tell the others were as well.

5

"I really *am* sorry," Jonathan said out loud as we dragged ourselves down the sidewalk.

"For fartin' on my damn head?!" Kurt snapped at him.

"I only farted *near* you," Jonathan corrected.

"I don't give a *shit*!" Kurt yelled, then spotted a small bottle of body spray that had rolled onto the sidewalk. It came from a boutique store that had gotten its windows smashed, glass and products scattered around the ruined storefront. Kurt snatched up the bottle and began spraying himself. "And I don't care if I gotta smell like--" He paused to read it. "*'Cinnamon & Apple Pie'*, just as long as I don't smell like your *ass crack*!" He even sprayed his hair, shook his dreads out, then took a deep breath. "Ahhh. Much better. This stuff actually smells pretty good! Want some?" He held it out to me, grinning.

"I'm okay, Kurt. Thanks. You've sprayed *more* than enough around for *all* of us to enjoy the scent."

He tucked the bottle in his back pocket, then looked around on the ground for some more. He grabbed another random one, sprayed it into the air, and took a whiff. Kurt made a noise of delight, then read the bottle. "Ooo! *'Caramel & Buttered Popcorn'*! This tastes good enough to *eat*!" He pocketed that one, too. I groaned and shook my head.

"Dude, stop five-finger-discounting stuff!" Jonathan said to him, smirking.

"Due to current conditions, I *seriously* doubt what I'm doing will be cause for *arrest*," he retorted. "Everything's already on the ground anyway, so there!"

We hadn't even bothered to stop and wait for Kurt. Finally, he quit looking around for more bottles so he could catch up to us.

The remaining *recent* dead that had been attacked by tainted people were still getting up and staggering around the littered streets. We did out best to keep ourselves off Germantown Ave. by dodging between more store buildings and homes. I hoped regular people wouldn't try to attack us, thinking *we* were tainted, especially since we were skulking across their property. But, if they were smart, they'd stay inside. I kept my hand over the top of the soda can, not wanting to spill its contents.

Fire trucks were in a few locations, trying to help the cops round up the dead bodies. Shooting them with bullets didn't work, so they were trying another forceful tactic---shooting them with blasts of water. It looked almost pitiful seeing those disheveled, defenseless, dead beings get pushed back by the force of the water, only to smash into buildings and crack apart into little pieces.

Laughter. We looked around, puzzled, even though I had a feeling who it was.

Ock was lounging back in someone's lawn chair, legs crossed, enjoying a mixed drink in a tall, skinny glass, complete with a little umbrella and maraschino cherry. He had a red suit on this time.

"What a romp *indeed*," he said, his creepy eyes flashing in the dark. "I haven't had this much fun in *eons*!"

I felt like I had swallowed a lump of ice that sat in the pit of my stomach. I hoped Ryan wouldn't be able to feel that.

"C'mon, boy! Think up another good wish! I *know* you can!" Ock taunted Jonathan. "One more, and who knows? Maybe you'll have the whole world cave in on itself! Wouldn't ***that*** be a blast!"

Wishing he'd shut up, I flung some of the water at Ock. Red splotches formed and bubbled on his skin where the water hit. He screamed, then disappeared.

"Christine!" Jonathan said, worried about what I just

did.

"Don't worry, we still have plenty left for his banishing."

"So Miss C, how exactly are we gonna catch that little rat-fink?" Kurt asked me. "If he can appear and disappear at will…"

"But if I know Kiera, I bet she'll be able to find some sort of spell to track him down."

Kim looked at the sky. "Oh no."

The rest of us looked up. The sky was a dull shade of blue. Sunrise was coming.

More spirits than ever were floating through the air. Against the blue color of the sky, the specters looked like dark wisps of gray. Some had manifested into more solid forms than others, but the fact remained, they were disquieted by the current events.

Among the ghostly floating masses, it looked like some birds were flying in an unorganized group. But as they approached us, they looked *way* too thin to be birds, or any other type of *living* creature.

The paper bats had returned.

Kurt snorted. "Like those things can harm us."

Agreeing in unison, we kept walking, unfazed by their frenzied approach. Then Jonathan started yelling when they swarmed around us.

"Ow! Ow! *Paper cut*! ***Paper cut!***"

Kim snickered, but then he started yelling too, smacking them away from him.

"AHH! That shit *burns*!"

He was right. A paper wing sliced my cheek, and it felt like someone put lemon juice on my wound. I yelled and covered my cheek with my hand.

"What the *hell*?!--" I started angrily.

Kurt was shrieking, swinging his arms everywhere,

trying to keep the bats away. I concentrated on a single thought, and in seconds, every bat ignited on the spot and dropped to the ground, leaving their charred, papery remains behind. They stared at the ashes for a second, then we hauled ass to the mansion.

Once we were there, I noticed the girl that Dracula Dude had bitten had disappeared. So did the chewed-up looking guy who had grabbed Jonathan's pant leg. Dracula Dude himself was still asleep on the sidewalk. We ignored him and went inside.

Kiera, Dino, and Dennis were on the couch, reading through more of her books.

"You're back!" Kiera got up, rushing to us to give us hugs again. She pulled me towards where she was sitting. "I was getting a little worried. Any luck?"

Silently, I handed her the can of holy water, then collapsed on the couch next to Dennis. He rubbed my shoulder. Kurt sat on the loveseat, Kim beside him. Jonathan eased himself into a chair, noticing that Dino was eyeing him awful hard.

"Stupid fuck, wishing for *Halloween* every day," he grumbled.

Jonathan frowned. "How 'bout I pull your arm out of its socket and beat you over the head with it?"

"I'd like to see you try, you Robert Smith reject."

"Yo, you shut up," Kurt snapped at Dino. "Like Miss C said, none of us knew that this shit was gonna happen."

"And we *must* work together in order to banish Ock," I continued. "So no playing the blame game."

"There's a spell in here that can summon any lower demon you choose," Kiera said, showing me one of her hardback books. She pointed to the sigil that one would need to call forth a demon.

"Is it kinda like what we did for Ryan when *he* was

possessed?" I asked her.

"Not exactly. The sigil's different, of course, and we need to lure him in somehow, with some sort of sacrifice."

"Sacrifice?!" Kurt exclaimed, sitting up. "Like, *kill* something and offer it to him?"

"A sacrifice doesn't *always* have to be something killed," she said quickly, to ease his mind. "Just something he might really like, to appease him while we have him."

"But…won't he recognize *us* trying to summon him?" Dennis asked, scratching his head.

"Spiritual dimensions are a little weird," Kiera said. "Whatever realm he's running around in at the moment, *our* realm looks different to him from where he is--until he's actually *in* it."

"Like being in a thick fog and not knowing a tree is in front of you until you smack into it?" Kurt offered.

Kiera snickered. "Yeah, something like that. Ock might see the offering, but not see who's giving it to him, and where it's coming from…until it's too late, of course." She took the big book off my lap, and handed me her great-great grandmother's book of spells, which smelled like mildew. She pointed to another sigil.

"*That's* the entrapment sigil, the same one we used on Our Lord. We'll use that to bind Ock here when we summon him, so we can end his farce."

"Hmm…since we need two sigils, how is this gonna work?"

"The summoning circle has to be on the ground, and I figure we can hover the trapping sigil *above* him, like a tent, almost."

Dennis looked like he was in thought. "Maybe use a sheet? We could hover *that* over him."

"Good idea," Dino said. "Let's look for one." The two of them dashed upstairs.

I sighed and leaned back on the couch, closing my eyes. Actually, we all were silent for a moment, trying to recuperate.

A scream from outside startled us from out of our meditation. We got up to see what was wrong.

We peeked out of the window next to the front door. The sun was up now, and Dracula Dude was awake, fanning himself with his cape. White tendrils of smoke emanated from him as he did a crazy dance, still flapping the cape around. Then, without warning, he burst into flames.

He continued running around the lawn, yelling in pain, until he exploded into a pile of ashes. Kiera and I gasped, covering our mouths. Kurt's jaw dropped, and Jonathan and Kim yelped in surprise.

"Did he just go, '***POOF***'?!" Kurt exclaimed, wide-eyed. Dino and Dennis had come back down the stairs, Dino holding a folded up sheet in his hand.

"Spontaneous human combustion! Friggin' ***awesome***!" Jonathan blurted out.

"Who spontaneously *what*?" Dino sounded confused.

"You know, *spontaneous human combustion*!" Jonathan stated, as if Dino should have known. "One of those weird-ass, unexplained phenomena, like UFOs, Bigfoot, Loch Ness, werewolves, Chupacabra…well, with SHC, a person can just burst into flames with no logical explanation as to *why*. Google it." Jonathan concluded and grinned.

Dino frowned at him. "What the *fuck* is a *Chupacabra*?" he asked, irked that Jonathan just schooled him.

"It's the Spanish word for '*goat sucker'*," I answered, still staring out of the window, watching something *very* freaky happen.

"Who the *fuck* would wanna suck on a *goat*?!" Dino continued. No one answered him. Everyone was just as engrossed with what was going on outside as I was.

The ashes of Dracula Dude were *gathering*, looking like

little insects crawling across the lawn, trying to *find* each other.

"Hole...eee...*crap*," Kiera whispered. Dino and Dennis wedged themselves between us to see what we were gawking at.

The ashes continued regrouping themselves, creating a human-like form. Then they darkened, looking wet, coming into shape. It was like watching one of those fast-motion clips of something decaying…but in reverse.

Bone, then red muscle, tissue and organs reconstructed themselves in a matter of seconds. Lastly, skin formed over the meaty carcass.

Naked, Dracula Dude opened his eyes and stood up. Then, white smoke wafted from his skin. He screamed as he burst into flames, ran around, flailed his arms, then exploded into ashes---*again*.

The boys gasped, frozen in awe.

"No…fucking…*way*." Jonathan's jaw dropped next, but he looked more fascinated than terrified.

"He's in the *sun*," I started. "As long as he stays there, *that's* going to keep happening to him. Remember, no one's gonna die now, since Jonathan's new wish is in effect."

"But, that's *torture*!" Dino gestured out the window to the reforming body.

"And we're gonna keep hearing him scream, over, and over, *and over*, if we don't get him into some shade," Kiera said.

"But the dude is *nuts*! He thinks he's *Dracula*! Hell, he ***is*** Dracula!" Kurt grabbed Kiera's arms. "You really think he's gonna be all nice and *civil* towards us?!"

"Well, what do you propose we do? Keep listening to him scream every other minute, or put him somewhere dark?"

We watched as the guy's shrieking, naked, flaming body crazily ran across the lawn once again. Jonathan started chuckling to himself.

"That shit's starting to look *funny*," he said between giggles. Kurt popped Jonathan in the back of his head.

"Heyyy! What was *that* for?"

"That's also a *human being*, albeit it a loony one." He sighed. "Alright, let's find a way to stash him somewhere until this mess is over."

"How about the horse stalls?" I suggested. "They're pretty dark, and away from the sunlight."

"Good idea," Kiera said. "But the big problem is getting him *out* of the sunlight before he bursts into flames again."

We gotta try to shield him from the light while he's reforming, I guess." Dino hunched his shoulders.

"But once he reforms, won't he try to attack us?" Dennis asked.

"Ooo! I'll be back." Jonathan ran upstairs. He returned with three Gothic-looking crosses on chains, two small hand-held crucifixes, a Celtic cross wall mount about two feet in length, and a flat, brown, plastic cross hanging from a black cord, which suspiciously looked like it came from a cheesy monk or priest Halloween costume.

Grinning, he shoved the items at us.

Kiera gave sigh of disbelief and folded her arms. "You've *gotta* be kidding me."

"Hey, whatever works," I said, taking the wall mount. "At this stage in the game, *anything's* liable to work."

Kurt took a necklace and dangled the pendant in front of his eyes. "This cross has got a *skull* on it," he snapped.

Jonathan rolled his eyes. "It's a *cross*. Right now, that's all that matters!"

"Where'd you get all these necklaces from, anyway?" Kurt continued, not letting him off the hook. "Don't say the Halloween store."

"Actually, I got them at *Hot Topic* in the mall. The same time I got Christine's and Kiera's presents."

"Like *that* makes it any better," Kurt fussed.

"You went to a *mall*?!" Dennis asked, surprised, remembering Jonathan's mild agoraphobia. "Wow! Way to go, man!"

"Hey, I *like* that store!" Jonathan shot back at Kurt.

"Guys, guys, enough," I said. "Just take something and let's---" We heard screaming outside again. "Quick! Let's go out and wait for him to turn into dust."

Dino grabbed the plastic cross, and Kiera and Kim got the crucifixes. Jonathan, Kurt, and Dennis wore the necklaces.

We watched as the ashes made their way to each other, and we crept up on them, watching in amazement. Kurt and Jonathan had the sheet ready. When the ashes started forming a human shape, they held the sheet up to block the sun. I held the wall mount close to the head of the form, as did Dino with his plastic cross. Kiera and Kim stood a couple of feet behind us, crucifixes poised and ready.

Now that we were this close, we could actually *hear* his body reforming. Cracks, pops, crackling and crunches…and then the wet, sticky sounds of everything else. We all had grimaces on our faces.

"Good thing he doesn't *reek*," Jonathan said, his upper lip curled in a slight sneer.

"Aw, man! Now we're gonna to see his *junk*." Dino scowled in disgust.

"Ew! I don't wanna see some dude's *balls*!" Jonathan started freaking out, jumping up and down in place. Kurt shot him a look.

"Guys, *shut **up***!" Kiera stared at them in wonder. "There are things *way* more important right now than worrying about seeing some guy's privates!"

"Look!" Dennis pointed at the body. "Get ready!"

Dracula Dude opened his milky blue eyes and hissed at us, bloody fangs jutting from his mouth. I shoved the wall mount in his face and he hissed, crawling backwards. As soon as he was out of the shadow of the sheet, he started smoking. He shrieked and came back towards us.

"Yeah, that's right, *punk*," Dino said. "You *need* us *now*, you fang-toothed fucker."

Dracula Dude hissed at him, so Dino shoved his plastic cross in DD's face. DD cringed away, but still within the confines of the shade. He looked at all of us, confused, his eyes shifting to all the religious objects surrounding him, then to the sheet that Jonathan and Kurt were holding up for him. For now, DD kept still.

"Alright, what's next?" Kim asked. "It seems like we've got him under control."

"We'll have to lead him to the stable behind the house," Kiera said. "Let's move back slowly; take the shade away from him."

As a unit, we all stepped back. In the sun once more, DD started his antics all over again until he scrambled to get under the shade. He panted, then hissed at us, but immediately stopped when Dino, Kim, Kiera, Dennis and I held our crosses and crucifixes in front of him.

And so, we continued this strange ritual, easing backwards a little at a time, as DD slowly followed us under the shade of the sheet, leading him to the stables.

"Awesome. This is gonna work!" Jonathan said cheerfully.

"Hey! You, over there!" came a voice in the distance. We looked.

A cop car had pulled up, and two officers were coming towards us.

"Oh, come the hell ***on***…" My voice dripped with anger. "Not *now*!"

"We have this under control!" Kiera said firmly, hoping to keep the cops at bay.

Kurt groaned. "I swear, they're more of a *hindrance* than a *help* right now."

"It's not like they know what we are, or what we're capable of doing," Jonathan said. "We'd better play it cool."

"Seriously, ***we've got this***," I called to the cops.

"Who is that?" one of them asked, keeping some distance between themselves and us at first.

"Um, one of the psychotic people," Dino answered.

The other cop took out his handcuffs and walked towards DD.

"I wouldn't do that," Kiera quickly warned him. "He's very dangerous!"

"Let *us* handle this, miss," the first one said, sounding a bit cocky, ignoring her. "We'll take it from here."

"No," I answered curtly. "You *don't* want to do that."

He looked at me closer, then to Kim, Jonathan, and Kurt. "Wait a minute---you're all the ones who broke into the church!"

"Look, *occifer*, we ain't got *time* for this!" Kurt exclaimed.

Annoyances, annoyances! Why couldn't the humans just leave us *alone*?!

The second cop reached over to push DD onto his stomach so he could cuff him from behind, but DD grabbed his arm and squeezed. We heard the snap, and the bone from the cop's forearm punctured his flesh, and ripped through his shirt. A dark, red stain quickly began spreading on his sleeve. The cop screamed and fell to the ground in shock. Immediately, DD lunged over the cop and bit into his neck. Blood spewed from his carotid artery like a red fountain. The first cop opened fire on DD, putting three rounds into his back. DD jumped up and lunged for the other cop, biting into *his* neck as well. The cop gurgled, pushed DD away, and held his neck, blood seeping between his fingers.

"Shit!" I said, then motioned like I was grasping at the air. DD received the energies of my actions and started wheezing. He fell to the ground, choking, clawing at his throat, looking panicked. I spread my energies around him, forcing him to keep still.

"Dino, cuff him, quick," I said calmly, continuing to focus on DD. Dino snatched the handcuffs off the grass, then kneeled down to cuff DD's wrists.

"Okay…Kurt, Jonathan, cover him up and get him to the stables. Lock him up tight."

"Okey-doke," Jonathan replied. They spread the sheet on the ground, placed DD onto it, folded a corner of the sheet over him, then continued rolling DD forward until he looked like he was wrapped up in an oversized burrito. Once that was done, they dragged DD across the lawn, hissing and growling all the way.

I looked at the rest of the gang. "My guess is that the cops might turn into vampires as well." I looked at the two unmoving bodies, then to the squad car. "Lets put them in the back seat."

Kiera and I got the cop with the broken arm, and Dino and Kim got the other one. We picked them up and carried them to the car. Dennis found the cop's gun on the grass and brought that with him, holding it by using a tissue he had in his jacket pocket.

We set the cops down gently, and with a thought, I got the back door to unlock. I yanked the car keys off one cop's belt before we heaved their bodies onto the back seat, and Dennis tossed the gun in behind them. I gasped in surprise, and looked at him.

"Did you put the safety lock on *first*?"

He hunched his shoulders, and I sighed, holding my head for a moment. "Well, thank goodness it didn't go off."

"They'd come back to life again if they got hit by bullets

anyway," Dino said, waving it off. "No big deal."

Kiera groaned. "*Dino*! It's the *principle* of the matter!"

I slammed the car door shut. "At least when they come to, they won't be able to harm anyone." I tossed the keys in the front seat, then spotted a pen and notebook on the dashboard. I reached in and grabbed them, then wrote, "COPS IN BACKSEAT BIT BY HUMAN DRESSED AS DRACULA. ONE HAS INJURED FOREARM." I put it back on the dashboard so someone could see it through the windshield.

Kurt and Jonathan came running across the grass.

"All done!" Kurt said, grinning. "And if by chance he really *can* fly, he won't be able to flap his dumb, bat-ass anywhere."

"Thank you so much," I said, smiling. "Now, back to banishing Ock." I looked at Kiera. "How'd finding the lilacs and hyssop go?"

"The hyssop, surprisingly, we were able to find at the florist's," she started. "Lilacs, on the other hand, are bushes, and you can't find those at a flower shop."

Kurt sighed. "So now what?"

"Lets go back into the house, and gather what we have," I said. "We'll need a new sheet, and we need to draw the entrapment sigil on it. We also need a mirror, and to put the holy water in a different container. Don't forget the spell books. We'll just have to drive around now, and hunt down the lilacs ourselves."

"But, it's Fall! Lilacs are out of season! How are we gonna find a lilac bush if we can't spot its purple flowers?" Dennis asked.

"Leave *that* to me," Kim said and beamed. "Nature boy, remember?"

"Of course," I said and grinned. "Alrighty guys, time to hustle."

6

Ryan had a large, old, vanity mirror with an ornate wooden frame stashed away in his attic. I carefully brought that downstairs with me. Dino and Dennis were working on painting the sigil on the sheet, and Kiera had transferred the holy water into a small, clear, plastic bottle. Kim put the spell books in a book bag and slung it over his shoulder. Kurt and Jonathan were talking amongst each other, deciding on where to perform the rituals.

"I know of one cool place; it's outside *and* secluded."

"Where at, though?"

"It's pretty close, actually. It'd be nice not to have to go too far." He yawned. "I'm ready to *crash*."

"Oh no you don't," Kurt said, shaking him. "If *we* don't sleep, *you* don't sleep, either."

Jonathan stretched and yawned again.

"I'm not quite sure of the name of the street, but I can direct you there when we leave."

"Which means we have to drive around in the hearse," Kiera said and growled under her breath. "Kurt's car is too small for *all* of us. Those zombies better not mess up my paint job."

"So, it's the lilacs and open-land searching we have left to do," Kim said, rubbing his hands together. "Cool."

When the sheet was done, we carried it outside. It took a half hour for it to dry, which gave us a little time to rest. I was the only one who couldn't quite take a nap. I was still concerned that the news about what was going on here in Chestnut Hill would somehow get back to Ryan in Harrisburg. I wondered what he'd say. I didn't want him leaving his business trip on account of us, or thinking we couldn't take care of ourselves. But since I hadn't gotten a mental message from him yet, I figured we were still in the clear.

We peeked outside of the house before leaving. Not seeing anyone, we dashed to the hearse. Kurt jumped in the driver's seat, and Kim sat up front with him. The rest of us piled up in the back. I snickered at Kiera's bumper sticker, which read, *Come to the dark side…we have cookies.*

"You guys comfy?" Kiera asked.

"Yeah, *plenty* of room," Dino answered. "Although I never thought I'd *ever* ride in the back of a hearse…while *alive*."

Kiera rolled her eyes.

Jonathan crawled up to the front of the hearse and hovered behind Kurt and Kim's seats.

As Kurt drove, a barrage of psycho clowns came towards us, groaning and moaning, banging on the hood, trunk and windows in the usual, clichéd, zombie-like fashion. All we could see was a hideous medley of rainbow-colored stripes, polka dots, harlequin prints, pom-pom balls, jingle bells, and badly painted faces, which they were all too happy to press against the windows, leaving white, red, and black smears on the glass. One even had a red, Styrofoam, oversized baseball bat, hitting the driver's window. He wasn't harming the hearse, but Kiera didn't see it that way.

“***Get away from my car***!” she yelled at them. “You stupid **dorks**!”

“AAAHH! **CLOWNS**! *GO AWAY*!” Dennis covered his eyes, pressing his back against the car’s interior. “I ***hate*** clowns!”

Well, that left us with *one* man down when it came to defense, so the rest of us used our powers to either zap, toss, or push back the tainted humans as Kurt tried driving slow to avoid hurting anyone.

I noticed Dino giving Dennis a devious smirk. I had a funny feeling Dennis would *not* hear the end of his little clown phobia.

Once the tainted humans were dealt with, Jonathan gave Kurt various instructions as to where to make a left or right turn on certain streets. Shortly, we were traveling down a rather woodsy road that didn’t look too busy at the moment. Considering it was still relatively early in the morning, that was good. Kim had the window rolled down with his head sticking out of the car like a typical dog. It looked like he was sniffing the air.

“Wow, he can *still* smell lilacs despite them being out of season?” I asked.

“He told me a long time ago that every living thing has its own ‘vibration’, even plants. He must know what a lilac’s vibration is,” Kiera told me.

“There it is!” I heard Jonathan say, pointing up the road. “You might have to park on the side street.”

Kurt made a left turn, parking the hearse on a neighborhood block. We all crawled out of the back, while Kim and Kurt got out from the front. What a scene *we’d* make if anyone watched. We quickly crossed the road and stood before what was once an old house. I couldn’t tell if it was colonial or not, but my guess was that it might have been from the late 1800’s or 1900’s.

“Whoa, check *that* out,” Dennis said to himself. Dino looked mildly amused.

“Wow, I’ve *never* noticed that sitting along this roadside before,” Kiera said.

“Probably ‘cause it was covered in so much green, but since it’s fall now…” Kurt shrugged. “Well, c’mon, we ain’t got all day.” And so, hearing that, we trekked up the beaten dirt path.

Looking around the ruined shell, I was awed at the leftover stone structure. The remnants of a stair case, and even a fireplace was there. I also saw that what was left of the windows had some sort of screen still attached. Then I noticed a glass beer bottle and a couple of soda cans on the flooring.

“Obviously, this must be a hangout spot,” I said dryly, kicking the bottle. I listened to the clinking noise it made as it skittered across the old stones.

“But isn’t it *cool*?” Jonathan was beaming. “It looks all creepy and scary and everything!”

“Well, I’ll give ya *that* much. It *is* cool and creepy looking, but really crappy to do the ritual in.” Kiera folded her arms.

“Aww, *why*?” He pouted like a disappointed, little kid.

“Well, for one, see how close to the road it is?” Kurt gestured to the street. “Just any ‘ol body can come driving down this road and see us moving around in here! We need to be *away* from prying eyes. God forbid they call the cops. We really don’t need *them* interfering any more in our business today.”

“And the spell requires us to be in an *open field*, remember?” I added.

“Yeah. No special effects needed to send that little goat-bastard to hell,” Kurt continued. “Just the bare necessities.”

Without warning, Kim took off behind the ruins.

“What--?” I started.

“Maybe he found some lilacs!” Kiera gave a hopeful smile.

About ten minutes later, Kim emerged from the woods with a huge branch in his hand. It was covered with leaves which shook in the wind as he ran back towards us.

“Ta-daaa!” he said happily, shaking the branch. “One more chore on the list to go!”

"Now we gotta go to a park somewhere," Dino said. "But where's a place a whole lotta people *won't* be at?"

Dennis looked to the ground. "That definitely leaves Valley Green out. People are *always* wandering all over the place through there---biking, walking, jogging…"

"It has to be some place *away* from Fairmount Park. We gotta get *off* the beaten track," I ran a hand through my hair. "And do it fast. The longer we go searching, the less time we'll have to set up everything and summon Ock."

"Well, let's hop to it, gang!" Kurt waved us back to the hearse, Kim slinging the branch over his shoulder as we walked.

Kiera helped Dennis and Dino strip the leaves off of the lilac branch, and Jonathan and I took care of the hyssop. We placed everything into two gallon-sized, Ziploc bags.

"*High noon*," Kurt blurted out as he drove, then snorted. "What the *hell* kind of ritual requires being done in the middle of the *day*? Do you know how *tough* it's gonna be finding a spot unoccupied by people at that time?"

"That's probably why Ock's banishing is so tricky," Kiera said. "Ock thinks he's slick."

For nearly an hour, we kept driving, looking out of the windows for any possible place to set up camp. We went as far as New Britain, PA before Kiera's face lit up.

"There's a park around here… Peace Valley, I think," she said excitedly. I looked up from the spell book I was reading. Dino, Dennis, and Jonathan had zonked out, but woke up when they heard her voice. "Yes! I vaguely remember this area. I came here to visit my grandma during the summers when I was really little. There's water around here somewhere."

"Get your bearings and point me in the right direction," Kurt replied, sounding eager.

Kim stuck his head out of the window again, closing his eyes, drinking in the fall air.

"She's right. I *can* smell the water."

"You *can*?" Jonathan asked him. "*I* can't smell a thing!"

Kim touched his nose and grinned.

"Show-off," Jonathan mumbled.

Kim pointed up a road, and Kurt followed his directions. Sure enough, we came to a *huge* park, complete with river. There were plenty of parking lots, but the most important thing was, there were barely any cars around.

Kiera opened the back door to the hearse. "This might be our lucky day, guys!"

"It'd *better* be," Dino grumbled. "I don't wanna deal with any more costumed freaks on a *daily* basis."

We practically tumbled out of the car, stiff, tired, and very anxious. Grabbing our paraphernalia, we stood under the shade of a tree.

"Okay, where to next?" I asked.

Kiera took a deep breath and slowly looked around. The lone cry of a bird sounded. Dennis was mesmerized by the sunlight sparkling off of the water.

"That area over there is a good start," she said, pointing

towards a woody area alongside a walking path. "I see a hidden trail. Hopefully it'll lead us deeper into the woods and to a clearing."

"Whoa, whoa, whoa," Kurt started. "You ain't say we had to go trekking *into* Mother Nature, you just said we had to find a clearing!"

"But we have to go *through* her to get *to* the clearing," Kiera replied. "Duh."

"But now we gotta deal with gnats and bugs and shit!" he protested. "They get on my nerves! Kurt does *not trek* through Mother Nature! I *know* my boundaries! She don't bother me, and I don't bother *her*. Simple!"

"You will if you want Halloween to stop going on *every single day*." Kim gave him a knowing look.

Kurt glowered at Jonathan. "Damn you and your wish shit."

"I thought Christine said no playing the *blame game*," Dino retorted.

Kurt fumed and pointed at Dino as if to tell him to shut up, and silently began stomping towards the hidden trail.

The seven of us walked together, the morning not even feeling like it was Halloween all over again. Being out this far away from city streets put us in a different mind-frame.

Dennis continued admiring the scenery, holding the folded sheet to his chest as we walked through the low-cut grasses. Jonathan sighed in contentment and took a few deep breaths of fresh air. Kiera tightly held the bags of lilac and hyssop, her focus more on what we had to do next. I held one spell book, while Kim held the other. Dino carried the mirror. Kurt was actually ahead of us, frowning all the way. He stumbled on a rock and cussed at it, then frantically started waving his arms back and forth, trying to keep the insects away from him.

"Ha!" Jonathan suddenly said. "If you didn't use so

much Apple Cinnamon spray, or whatever the hell it was, the bugs wouldn't be bothering you right now."

"Shut ***up***," Kurt replied in a dark tone, waving his arms again in anger. "If it wasn't for your foul-smellin' ass, I never would have had to *use* it!"

Finally, we came to the hidden trail.

Kurt stopped short and gawked at it.

"You see that? It's *dark* up ahead! *Dark* in broad *daylight*!" He swatted at a wasp that got too close to him. "Look at all these damn bees flying around! All these *weeds*!" Panicking, he started checking his pants. "And what about ticks and fleas and shit?!"

"That's why we're wearing *pants*. Just in case," Kiera said. "Now, get moving! It's already ten-thirty!" She gave him a little shove, and Kurt sucked his teeth, continuing on.

"Cool. I feel like I'm on a field trip!" Jonathan said, plucking a big, fat, white mushroom and observing it closely. He sniffed it and stuck out his tongue, not liking its smell, and chucked it into the grass.

"What about *animals*?" Kurt asked Kiera, wide eyed. "Raccoons! Deer! *Snakes*!"

"Deer will run from you! And stop worrying about stuff! You *can* defend yourself from anything, remember?!"

He paused. "Sometimes, I forget."

"Don't feel bad, Kurt, even I still do," I said, then turned to Kim. "You think we're going in a good direction?"

"Definitely. A few more minutes, and we *should* come to a clearing."

Kiera looked at Kurt. "Ha!" she said, imitating Jonathan, and he rolled his eyes.

Kurt took a few more stumbles and nearly twisted his ankle on an exposed tree root, now cussing the tree out. Almost as if in reply, a gnat flew right into his eye, and he inhaled a small green, flying insect.

"GODDAMN *BUGS*!" he screamed, immediately trying to shoot the bug back out of his nose with short, forceful exhales.

"Ew! Snot rockets!" Jonathan said and laughed, then he got a bit of payback. Another gnat flew into his mouth, and he started spitting and wiping his tongue off with his t-shirt. Then he got hit in the forehead by a big, green, June bug.

"Ow! Those things hurt," he mumbled, rubbing his sore spot. "Dumb beetle!"

"It's not like it hit you on *purpose*," Kiera said. "Ever see how tiny their little, beetle-heads are? They probably can't see too good."

Kim darted a few yards ahead of us. "Guys! We found it!"

We picked up our pace, following after Kim. The sight we saw was breathtaking.

Standing under a tree, we looked ahead. A clearing, and still green! It sloped downward, giving me the urge to run across it.

I wondered if Jonathan read my mind, because he did *exactly* that. He rushed past us, yelling, "Whoo-*hooo*!"

If the rest of us weren't bogged down with stuff, we might have chased after him. The most we could do was walk faster.

When it felt right to her, Kiera stopped. "Here is good," she said to us, and we put everything down. She sat cross-legged on the ground, and the rest of us followed suit. Jonathan laid back instead, folding his hands across his chest, looking up at the clouds.

Kiera flipped through her book, found the summoning spell, then rummaged through her bag, pulling out some items, one of them being a quart-sized, plastic bag full of sea salt. Another item was a chunk of charcoal. She used that to draw a six-foot wide circle on the ground, then the arcane symbols within it. Once that was done, she spread the sea salt around the outer perimeter of the sigil.

"Just taking extra precautions," she told me.

Jonathan twirled a tapered candle between his fingers. "Kinda funny how we're summoning him only to *banish* him, huh?"

Dennis raised his eyebrows. "Interesting point," he replied.

Dino and Kurt unfolded the sheet, then Kurt slapped his forehead, remembering something.

"Oh *crap*! We don't have the offering, or sacrifice, or whatever you wanna call it."

Kiera gasped. "Guys, we gotta find something, *quick*."

"But what would he like?" Dennis asked. "He's a trickster demon, right? Maybe he'll like jokes, pranks, magic tricks."

"Do we have any of that stuff *on hand*?" Dino asked him. Dennis shook his head. "Okay then, think of something else!"

"Find a dead animal or something!" Kiera said. "We've got a little less than an hour left."

Kim started sniffing the air, then raced off again. Jonathan jumped up.

"I'm going wherever *he's* going." Jonathan ran after Kim, grinning. "Wait up!"

In the meantime, Kiera, Dennis and I placed the banishing materials around the circle, going over the plan.

"Okay, Miss C. I'll summon him while Kurt, Dino, Kim, and Dennis hold the trapping sigil over the summoning sigil. When Ock appears, he won't be able to get away. Then you'll begin the banishing incantation. The first thing to strike him with is the holy water. Then you'll move on to the hyssop, then the lilacs, then finish with the holy water again. Jonathan will hold the mirror in front of Ock, and then…it should be over."

I looked over the banishing ritual. "This stuff creeps me out a little."

She laughed. "*You*, having the powers of *Abraxas*, nervous about a little banishing spell?"

I smirked. "Thanks for reminding me. *Again*."

Kim and Jonathan were coming back with small things in their hands. I grimaced.

"Ugh. Don't tell me…"

"Yep," she answered, her tone flat. "They're holding dead things." She made a face. "I'll *never* understand how guys can just *do* that."

"What? Be gross?"

She nodded and snickered at me.

Kim and Jonathan dropped a stiff sparrow and a limp squirrel at our feet.

"Thank you guys," Kiera said, then wrinkled her nose. "Uck, they *reek*!"

"Think he'll like money?" Jonathan asked, taking a crumpled dollar bill out of his back pocket, and wrapped it around the bird. He asked Kurt for a rubber band, who took one out of his hair. Jonathan secured the dollar bill around the bird with that.

"Something is *seriously* ***wrong*** with you!" Dino said, sounding like he was in a daze as he stared at the bird, wide-eyed. "I can't *believe* you just did that! You really *are* screwed in the head." He paused. "Maybe I should just stop fuckin' with you *altogether*."

Jonathan smirked at him, then gave the bird to Kiera. She held it with her thumb and index finger like it was diseased, and placed it in the center of the summoning circle. Using a tissue, she placed the squirrel next to the bird.

“Okay, what’s the time now?” Kiera asked no one in particular.

Kurt looked at his watch. “Shit, it’s eleven-forty five already.”

She took a deep breath, centering herself. Then she picked up her book and began speaking the summoning spell.

One thing about these summoning and banishing rituals, they involved *a lot* of repetitive words. There probably was a reason behind it, but still...

She continued speaking the conjuration over and over, until we caught the faint smell of sulfur---a sign that it was working.

Jonathan looked around. “Is it me, or is the sky getting darker?”

“Yeah, it looks like it’s gonna rain,” Dennis said. “Did anyone listen to the weather forecast?”

In minutes, the sky was a solid gray, looking like it was about to pour down any minute. I sensed it had to do more with Ock showing up than anything else.

The sulfur odor was getting stronger, the air feeling electric, smelling metallic. I started to get worried.

Kiera chanted furiously, and with each repeat of the invocation, her words sounded more demanding. The skies grew even darker, the winds churning. The guys held on as tight as possible to the sheet. A nervous energy vibrated through the group.

A small form began to materialize within the circle, transparent as a ghost at first, then became solid within a minute’s time. Ock seemed out-of-focus, shaking his head at first to get his bearings.

“What? Who summoned me?!” he said to himself, then looked up.

“You **stupid** *meat sacks*!” Ock yelled at us, then looked down at his feet, spotting the dead bird and squirrel. He laughed so hard, he fell on his ass, a big, wet spot forming in the seat of his pants.

"Incontinent much?" Jonathan said in a whisper. I pursed my lips together, not wanting to laugh.

"What the fuck is ***this***?!" Ock stood up and grabbed the dollar-wrapped bird. He flung it hard at Jonathan. It bounced off his chest and fell to the ground. Jonathan didn't even flinch.

"Why would I want something the Bossman already created to aid in your kind's corruption? Don't *insult* me." He picked up the squirrel and threw it at Kim. Fortunately, he dodged it. Otherwise, Kim might have gotten putrid squirrel guts on him.

"You *should* be checking out your precious little neighborhood," he said with a pointy grin. Everyone's still in a panic!" He put the back of his hand to his forehead, pretending to faint. "Oh, woe is me, woe is thee! Dumb, whiny *fucks*. I'm outta here!"

He tried to disappear, but something sent a jolt through his body, and he convulsed for a second. He tried vanishing again, and got the same reaction. He did it once more, and then, I saw it.

An invisible sphere was surrounding him. It became visible only for a split-second when he touched it. It reminded me of television static. He finally glanced up, seeing the sheet hovering above him.

Ock screamed at us, showing all his nasty, yellowed teeth.

I began the banishing incantation, and he started cursing at me, trying to distract me. I spoke louder and firmer, cutting out the sound of his voice.

He looked at Jonathan.

"Aw, c'mon, boy! You *really* wanna give up the chance to wish for ***whatever you want***?!"

"I'm *not* getting what I want! Every time I try to do

something good with my wishes, you twist them all around!"

"*Twist* them?! Don't be so dramatic! I was merely polishing 'em up for ya!"

Everyone sneered at Ock, and he cringed, sneering right back.

I tossed a bit of holy water on him, and like before, his skin blistered and smoked.

"FUCKING BITCH!" he screamed at me.

At that, I was half-tempted to kill him on the spot---but no, I would follow this ritual to the letter. Who knew *what* would happen if I strayed.

Kiera was by my side, holding open the bags of lilac and hyssop. As I chanted, I grabbed a handful of the leaves and threw them on Ock. Each leaf that touched him flared up on contact, burning holes of fire into him. He dropped to the ground, writhing in pain, rolling around and moaning. The smoke stung my eyes and the stench made me heave. I tossed the rest of the leaves on him, some of his flesh burning away into blackened, crusty chunks that cracked and peeled away with every move he made. Under the fleshy guise, his true skin color, a rancid, grayish-green color, slowly became exposed.

"Alright, alright! I'll make you a deal!" he yelled to Jonathan. "I won't interfere with any more wishes you make! Scout's honor!"

Jonathan laughed in his face. "You demons *have* no honor."

"Couldn't get *that* one past you, eh, Einstein?" He gave a maniacal laugh.

I kept chanting, Ock now looking like he was beginning to sink into the ground, as if he was in quicksand. He started screaming and yelling again, trying to distract my concentration, but all his follies weren't working. I took the whole bag of lilacs and dumped it on him. Now he looked like he was tarred-and-feathered. He threatened all of us with death next, which we already knew he wasn't capable of acting out on. I continued chanting, and Ock pleaded to Jonathan again.

"Look, I don't wanna go back *down there*, and you don't want Hell up here. Fine! How 'bout I just--?"

I was about to toss the last of the holy water at him, but Jonathan put his hand on mine. "Wait," he said to me. I paused and raised an eyebrow, wondering what Jonathan had up his sleeve.

"One more wish--and you CAN'T screw it up," he said to the demon. I gasped in horror. Everyone else looked at him like he had completely gone off his rocker.

Ock's eyes widened, looking hopeful.

Jonathan looked at all of us, gave me a slight nod with a grin, then took a deep breath before he spoke.

"I wish…for everything and everyone---***for the rest of their days***---to be ***exactly*** like how they were, as if they were ***not*** under any type of spell! That ***also*** means *not* having any memories of what happened to them while they were *under* said spells, either!"

Ock's eyes shifted from side to side, thinking hard, trying to find a loophole in Jonathan's wish. Not finding any, he hollered in frustration.

And, since his mouth was wide open, I gleefully tossed the last of the holy water into it.

The inside of his mouth gurgled and frothed into a bubbly, red mess, spilling down the sides of his chapped lips. The last vestiges of his skin disguise slid off and plopped to the ground like wet dough. His four arms reached out for us, his beady goat's eyes turning red and furious.

"Now, Jonathan!" I said. He picked the mirror up off the grass, then turned it around so Ock could see his reflection.

The demon gave off such an ear piercing screech, I thought I'd go deaf. The guys actually yelled in pain and almost let go of the sheet.

Ock began glowing brighter and brighter until he was as blinding as a lighthouse beacon. We turned our heads away, and Ock exploded in flash of white.

I peeked. Jonathan slowly lowered the mirror.

Aside from the sigil Kiera drew on the ground, everything looked completely untouched.

All of us cheered. Kiera and Jonathan jumped up and down, then we all crushed each other into one, big, group hug.

Ock would bother us no more.

Suddenly, Kurt broke away from us and started yelling and dancing around. He practically ripped the button off his pants trying to take them off. We stared at him in wonder.

He shoved his pants down to his ankles, then jumped out of them, rubbing his left butt cheek.

"Kurt! What the hell is wrong?" Kiera asked.

"Something was burning me!" he replied, then partially pulled down his tighty-whities so we could see. The boys immediately turned their heads away. "You see anything?!"

Kiera and I looked, then she chuckled. "Wow, Kurt, you actually have a little red mark--" She squinted harder. "Shaped like ***the key***!"

"Aw, holy hell!" Kurt replied, grabbing his pants to look at them.

There was a large, burnt hole edged with molten metal on his back pocket. I gasped.

"**That little goat-bastard!!**" Kurt yelled, balling his fist up at the sky. "He owes me ninety bucks for these pants!"

7

Dennis let Kurt borrow his jacket so he could tie it around his waist. However, it still didn't shield Kurt from the bugs. I suggested him envisioning a shield around himself, something that looked like insect netting. After a minute of focusing on that, he had no further complaints on the way back to the car. He only got one odd look from a person jogging with their dog as we passed the walking trail, but he didn't care. It wasn't like that person would see us again.

As we approached the hearse, Dennis blinked. "Hey, no smears on the car. Look!"

Sure enough, the hearse was spotless. We stopped in our tracks, staring at it for a moment.

"Whoa, now *that's* cool," Jonathan whispered, eyes wide.

Kiera had a big smile on her face, probably *very* thankful she wouldn't have to wash it when we got back home.

We sat in the hearse for a moment, to collect ourselves again. Once Ock was banished, the skies had cleared right up. Everything was peaceful and serene again, so we enjoyed the scenery for a while. The only one feeling uncomfortable was Kurt, simply because he was sans pants.

"You *can* still put them back on, you know," Kiera said with a grin.

Kurt looked pretty flustered. "But there's a ***big hole*** in the ***ass part***!"

"Just tie the jacket back around your waist to *hide* it," Jonathan suggested. Grumbling about having to wear raggedy clothes, Kurt got out of the car, and Kiera handed him his pants. Kurt did an extra-fast switch-a-roo and tied the jacket back around himself once they were on, still embarrassed about his scorched underwear plus the hole in his pocket, then hopped back into the hearse.

"So, you really think it's over? Is it officially November 1st?" Dennis asked.

"I sure *hope* so," I said. "But the car *is* clean. The only way to find out is to ask someone."

"I'll do it," Kiera said, getting out. She strolled over to a couple in the distance who were playing Frisbee with their dog. In a few seconds, she came back, running and smiling, her arms raised in victory. We all cheered again, giving each other high-fives.

"You worded that last wish *very* well." I hugged Jonathan to me. "I'm *so* proud of you."

Jonathan was beaming. "Thanks, Christine."

"The *true* test will be when we go through the neighborhood again," Kurt said. "Hopefully, it'll all look like nothing ever happened."

The drive back home was nearly silent. A lot of us had zonked out again; even I did every few minutes. Kurt alerted us when we were back in Chestnut Hill. We woke up and eagerly looked out of the windows.

The streets were clean. Everyone looked normal, going about their business. No ruptured cemetery. No smashed pumpkins. No dead bodies. No broken store windows.

Everything *was* back to normal.

Once again, the tension in the air lifted, and I was happy to see the cop car was gone from in front of the mansion as well. Even though I knew the cops' mishap was part of the debacle, it just felt *extra* good not seeing it there.

We went inside, our spirits high. Ryan would be home that afternoon, so we all promised to keep the entire incident a secret. Not that we *had* to---I just didn't need Ryan worrying about us when he went away on any more future business trips, or feeling bad that he wasn't there to help when stuff happened. Once more, we proved to ourselves that we could take care of whatever was dished out at us.

We all were in desperate need of a shower, so we retired to our respective rooms to get cleaned up, emerging later after a couple hours of some well-earned sleep.

It was finally sunset, and we all were sitting in the living room. Dino, Dennis and Kim were watching TV, Kurt was reading a magazine, and Kiera was jotting down some stuff in one of her notebooks, while I lounged across the couch. Jonathan was sitting on the floor, leaning his back against it. I propped my head on his shoulder to see what he was doing.

He was sorting out his candy, putting each specific type in its own pile. Chocolates in one, gum in another, and hard candies in a third. I sniffed and grinned, resting my head on a pillow.

After he divvied up the candy he earned himself, Jonathan dug through the remainder of his loot, and pulled out the extra trick-or-treat bag he found. He opened it, then made a face, unsure of something. Jonathan stuck his whole face back into the bag, then immediately withdrew, eyes shut tight, and coughing.

"Ugh! It smells like shit!" He tried handing it to me.

"*I* don't want it," I said, pushing it back, laughing. He tried passing it to Dennis next, who held his hands up and shook his head.

Kiera put her pen down and looked at him, rolling her eyes. "*Why* does it stink?" she asked.

Jonathan checked the outside of the bag, making sure it hadn't fallen into dog crap. Seeing it was clean, he looked in the bag again, then took out a small, round object. He held it up and looked at it really hard.

"No ***way***!" Jonathan said, still gawking at it.

"Wait a sec." Kurt looked at it too. "You mean to tell me… that's the *same* kid's bag you had stink-bombed earlier?"

"Ooo, talk about cruel irony," I replied.

Looking scared, he took out a miniature *Three Musketeers* bar and unwrapped it. Then he sniffed it before taking a bite. His expression looked relieved.

"Whew. At least it doesn't taste like how it smells," he quipped.

"Only *Jonathan* would *willingly* test that out!" Kim said and laughed. Dino rolled his eyes, shaking his head at them.

"Hey, why waste good candy?" Jonathan grinned, dumping the rest of the bag onto the floor to continue separating the loot.

I heard a key go into a lock. We lifted our heads to the sound.

"Remember, ***calm*** and ***cool***," Kurt told us.

Ryan stepped into the foyer, then looked in our direction, smiling. Everyone greeted him immediately.

"Ryan!" I exclaimed, jumping off the couch, rushing to him. He set his briefcase on the floor and spread his arms wide. I practically knocked him down as we collided.

He held me tight. "It feels *so* good to have you in my arms again, my love," he said, then held my face and kissed me. I wrapped my arms around him again and squeezed.

"Christine…" He took a deep breath, so I eased up on him. "I know you're glad to see me, but, you seem…*anxious*. Was everything alright while I was away? It was only two days---"

"Two days is too *long*," I said, giving him another kiss, running my fingers through his soft, salt-and-pepper colored hair.

Ryan smiled, then looked at my hand. His eyebrows came together in puzzlement.

"My dear, *what* is that gaudy thing 'round your wrist?"

"Oh," I whispered, waving it off. "Halloween present from Jonathan."

He snorted. "He's subjecting you to his little gifts now, I see. Well, at least Kiera won't be alone on that." Ryan smirked.

"Ah, no big deal. It was still a sweet gesture on his part."

"Hmm," Ryan replied, not sounding too happy as he pulled a curtain back to look out of the window beside the front door. I could tell he knew *something* had happened. "There weren't any pranksters lurking around, or pumpkin-throwing in the neighborhood, I hope."

Kurt let out a little squeak, and Kiera jabbed him in his ribs. Ryan gave them a curious look.

"Well, just a *little* bit," I said, digging the tip of my shoe into the floor.

"Did they damage anything around the house?"

"Oh, no, not at all! There wasn't any damage here.... *per se...*" I mumbled under my breath.

"My love," he said gently, taking my hands in his. "You're trembling, and your heart is *racing*. I feel it, and it's driving me crazy. What *happened* here?"

I took a deep breath. "Ryan, I'm just glad you're *home*," I answered honestly. "Safe and sound."

He took off his coat and put it in the coat closet. They watched him, grinning like Cheshire cats. Perhaps they were overdoing it.

"So," Ryan said, clapping his hands together and rubbing them. "What did you all do yesterday?"

"Trick or treating!" Jonathan said, cheerfully. Ryan raised an eyebrow at him.

"Son, you *still* go out begging for candy?"

"We had to get him out of the house *somehow*," Kim said. "I went with him. So did Kurt and Christine."

"How thoughtful," he said to us. "Did you go with him as well?" Ryan looked at Kiera, Dino, and Dennis.

"Well, there *was* a Halloween party going on at the

college campus. *I* went to that," she answered.

"And me and Dennis were just hanging out," Dino concluded. "Halloween's stupid anyway."

"Is not," Jonathan and I said in unison. We looked at each other and laughed. Kurt and Kiera rolled their eyes at us.

"I'm glad you all enjoyed yourselves," Ryan said. "The merger with my company and *Tek Technologies* overseas went very smoothly. I might have been home earlier if it wasn't for this." Ryan produced a long, skinny, black box from his back pocket and handed it to me.

"Ryan, you know I hate it when you do this." I gave the box a pitiful look.

"I wish you'd learn to love it," he said softly, embracing me from behind, then kissed my neck.

I opened the box, revealing a shiny necklace with a silver cross pendant. In the center of the cross was a glittering rose, tiny diamonds, no doubt.

"Ryan, this is *gorgeous*," I whispered, looking at him. His amber-green eyes twinkled in the light of the chandelier above. "Thank you." I gave him a big kiss.

A tiny 'awww' came from Kiera as Ryan slipped the necklace around my neck.

Ryan walked towards the kitchen next, and we followed tightly behind him. Even I had to admit, that looked pretty goofy, and I was glad Ryan didn't notice.

"I don't know about all of you, but I'm *famished*. What's everyone in the mood for?"

Two called out pizza, three called out Chinese, and Jonathan yelled out McDonald's.

"Like you need *another* cow burger cloggin' up your pipeline," Kurt said as he glared at Jonathan.

"I vote we all go out to a nice Italian restaurant, since everyone's not on the same page," Ryan answered with a quirky grin.

"Fine with me!" Jonathan said eagerly. Everyone else quickly nodded, and Ryan paused, staring at all of us again.

"Every single one of you is acting *very* peculiar, and I'd like to know *why*," he said, folding his arms, cocking an eyebrow in suspicion. "*What* are you all trying to hide from me?" Then, Ryan blanched. "I hope you didn't *surprise* me with something." He looked us each in the eye very carefully. "I'm not too fond of surprises."

"No, no surprise, My Lord," Kiera said quickly, as Ryan took a glass from the cabinet above the sink, and opened a bottle of brandy, pouring the glass a quarter full. He gave us a shifty look before taking a sip, and told everyone to get their coats. We exited the kitchen, still a little nervous. I glanced back at Ryan to notice he was still looking at us.

"Guys, *loosen up* before he worms the story out of one of us!" Kurt hissed.

"Deep breaths," I said. "That works wonders for me."

Jonathan started breathing deep, but after three exhales, he held his head. "Yeesh, that makes me dizzy!"

I snorted and looked to the ceiling.

We grabbed our coats, and I got Ryan's as well. Walking back to the living room, I peeked into the kitchen to tell him we were ready, but he wasn't there. I wondered where Ryan had disappeared off to, and *why*. I returned to the guys, looking puzzled, butterflies in my stomach. Something was up. I'd never seen Ryan vanish so quickly like that before.

"What's the matter, Miss C?" Kiera asked me, looking as worried as I was.

I got my answer in two seconds, as Ryan's voice boomed from *past* the stables, through the dining hall area, and into the living room, where we were.

"***CHRISTINE*! Why in *God's name* is there a terrified, *naked* young man in my *stables*?!**"

Wide eyed, we all looked at each other and cringed.

I paled, slapping a hand over my mouth in a complete, '*oh shit*' moment. Kiera, who was sitting on the arm of the couch, gave a little shriek, rolled her eyes, and fell back onto the cushions, covering her face. The guys groaned and lowered their heads, realizing our one-and-only mistake throughout this whole, ridiculous fiasco.

We had *totally* forgotten about the dude formerly known as Dracula.

"***Crap in a hat!***" Kurt said, throwing his arms up in the air, exasperated. I couldn't have said it any better myself.

"Make that, *steaming pile* of crap in a *stovepipe* hat!" Jonathan replied, running a hand through his purple-streaked hair, and giving me a grin before he burst out laughing.

Oh well, there went keeping our little haywire Halloween a *secret*, damn it…

JOIN THE CLAN…

Http://groups.yahoo.com/group/Gratista_Vampires

See what's in store for you.

ABOUT THE AUTHOR

A digital artist and still-photographer, Ms. Santiago is also Editor/Publisher of ***Dark Gothic Resurrected Magazine****--a 2nd place finalist in the* ***Preditors & Editors Readers Poll for 2008****--having created this publication to give new and unpublished writers and artists of the genre a chance to shine and see their names in print, preferring unique, edgy stories that are out-of-the-box. She also received the* ***Author's Site of Excellence Award*** *in December 2007 from* ***P & E****, and is a Cover Artist for* ***Damnation Books****.*

Http://groups.yahoo.com/group/Gratista_Vampires is an extension of DGR Magazine, where people of a like mind can join, share interests, network, and have the opportunity to be published in her group's bi-annual anthologies.

An avid fan of 'old school' horror movies (Freddy, Jason, Michael, Pinhead, etc.), Halloween is her favorite time of the year. She attended Community College of Philadelphia, majoring in English, with interests in creative writing and Theater. Ms. Santiago enjoys the Vampire/Goth scene and can be found haunting Philadelphia's "Dracula's Ball" from time to time, or roaming cemeteries and state parks. She has always been drawn to the flipside of life--the supernatural, odd, bizarre, Gothic and 'darkly beautiful' always being an inspiration to her.

She can be reached at GratistaVampires@yahoo.com, or http://bloodtouch.webs.com

www.ingramcontent.com/pod-product-compliance
Ingram Content Group UK Ltd.
Pitfield, Milton Keynes, MK11 3LW, UK
UKHW040558210726
13854UKWH00008B/1495

9 780557 060313